I0779387

SHERRI STEWART

Tricks and Treachery

By Sherri Stewart

ISBN-13: 978-1-959788-33-1

To my sister, Laurie, the real Leah of this story. Thank you for sharing your life with the readers of this book. It took courage to do so. You are missed. Perhaps the next time we meet, you can show me around heaven.

Chapter One

"Tricks and Treachery are the practice of fools that
don't have brains enough to be honest."
~ Benjamin Franklin

"Did you fall again?" Brynn Kingston asked the minute Leah, her sister, said hello. "What's up? Your message sounded urgent."

"Why do you always assume that there's something wrong, Brynn?"

Leah was right. Brynn was jumping to conclusions. Again. "Sorry. How are you doing today? You sounded upset. Is your rheumatoid arthritis kicking up?"

"No, actually, it's been easy getting out of bed and dressed all week, but I haven't done much except sit and watch TV. I was meaning to take a walk in the park this morning since the sun's out, but then I got lazy, and you know how that goes."

No, she didn't. From the moment Brynn woke to the time she fell into bed, she was running to catch up with all the work associated with running the Starlite Motel. What she wouldn't do to be able to sit at the pool and read a magazine. She bit her lip to keep from offering unsolicited advice. Leah couldn't help it if she was permanently disabled. On a bad day, she was as stiff as a board. She was doing the best she could. Leah just hadn't found her mojo yet.

"So what's wrong?" *Please hurry. I have to wash towels, place an ad for a new housekeeper since Ursula will be leaving for college in two days. Then there's the mountain of bills to climb.*

A sigh came through, loud and clear. "I have some news, but if you don't want to hear it—"

"No, tell me. I'm all ears."

"I just wanted to tell you that Gary asked me to marry him."

Silence. She didn't know how to respond. Gary. The phantom boyfriend whom her sister had never met, but who wanted to marry her, sight unseen. "Really? And did you say yes? I mean, you've never met him before."

Leah's voice took on a hard tone. "Yeah, but we've talked more than most couples have—every day for the last eight months."

"Married. Are you sure? When is all this going to happen?"

"When his contract is up with the oil rig at the end of this month. He'll have four weeks off, so he says he'll be flying from New Orleans to Michigan for the month. I know you're always so busy, but would you...consider being my maid of honor?" Leah's voice cracked.

How had they reached the point that Leah was afraid to ask her sister what should have been a no-brainer? "Of course, I'd be honored to be your maid of honor. You don't even have to ask." Brynn could almost feel the tension dissipate between them. "What kind of wedding are you planning?"

"Something last-minute, small, since I won't know much until he arrives. Gary won't have any family here, unless his daughter, Melanie, comes. I bought a wedding dress online. It's the kind I can wear for other occasions. I'll buy you your dress as well."

"Of course not, I'll buy my own dress, and it'll be nice to find one that I can wear again." Brynn's lips pressed so tightly together, it was causing her eyes to water. Leah's husband, Marty, had died in a car accident five years ago, leaving Leah a widow at twenty-five years old. She'd received an insurance check that helped her pay off their debts and provided her a bit of a cushion when she needed the money. Then Leah had been laid off when the moving company she worked for as a secretary downsized. She'd decided that she couldn't handle the walking and was happy to stay home.

Had she given the remains of her nest egg to the man named Gary, who promised to marry her? Was he one of those romance scammers she'd seen on *Dr. Phil*? But the minute she voiced her concerns, Leah always shut down like a frozen computer. This conversation needed to happen in person, where she couldn't hang up. "Leah, how would you like to go out to dinner? I could be in Grand Rapids in an hour. If I'm going to be your maid of honor, we need to do some planning."

A longer than needed pause preceded her sister's response. "All I can afford is fast food."

"I'll pay. How about Italian? You can show me

the dress you picked out, and I'd like to see what Gary looks like. How old did you say he was?" Brynn wasn't fooling her sister. Leah was street-smart. She'd have to walk on tenterhooks, or there'd be another argument, and Leah would become defensive.

"Sure. Give me two hours. I have to clean up the place before you come. Oh, he's on the line. Gotta go."

All right, she had two hours. First, she'd ask Milli to man the phones in the motel office. The clock read three-thirty, which meant people who didn't have reservations would see the vacancy sign and want to register for the night. Should she hang the No Vacancy sign since there were only two unoccupied rooms? Then she could lock the office and Milli could answer the phone from her house next door. No, Brynn needed the money. Summer was over, which meant unfilled rooms as the weather grew cooler.

A quick call, and Milli as usual was more than willing to fill in while Brynn drove from Saugatuck to have dinner with Leah. Milli was a godsend for all the times Brynn had to beat a path on I-96 to take care of family matters. She helped clean the rooms when the college intern didn't show up. Her husband, Brett, could fix a toilet, a broken air-conditioning unit, or a curtain rod at a moment's notice. And Milli was a wellspring of Biblical advice when Brynn's mind clouded with the urgent.

The drive to Grand Rapids was therapy, although the bumpiness of the road didn't help the car's alignment. It came to her halfway there. There was no Gary who lived in New Orleans and had a daughter and loads of money. And there was no Gary coming to marry Leah. So why had he asked her? To get her insurance money—that's why. And her sister wasn't going to give him up. She was hanging on to the matrimony rope with both fists. As long as he was a phone call away, there'd be no happy ending to this fairy tale.

Since her sister couldn't be convinced to give him up, Brynn had to expose him. But how? She'd seen the women—usually retired widows or divorcees who were victims of scammers. Like vultures, the scammers feasted on lonely women. Some of the victims, through tears, told of all the money that had drained out of their bank accounts. They'd learned the hard lesson only after the damage was done. But there were others who sat on Dr. Phil's bar stools, usually accompanied by their daughter or sister, who weren't willing to give up. They were holding out for the men who had stolen their hearts and pocketbooks.

Yes, she understood Leah's loneliness, the quiet of the house at night, the television providing the only sounds that broke said silence. She also understood the bleakness of a solitary future with no one to share the highs and lows of life.

There'd been a few potential men in her own life—a blind date that turned into a whirlwind of phone calls and outings, but he couldn't make the cut. Any potential husband of Brynn's had to love God first and her second. For all three of the guys she'd dated in college and in her twenties, they hadn't met the first requirement. Was there anyone out there who did? If so, she hadn't met him yet.

The motel kept Brynn busy when the house was too quiet. But Leah had no business to keep her busy, nor any interest in starting one. Gary was her business. And Brynn didn't foresee a happy reaction when she tore the bandage off the scab. But someone had to.

First, she'd listen. Ask questions. Look at pictures. Gather facts. Then she'd wait until they were in the car after eating dinner to inform Leah of her plan. Brynn was going to seek out an online company that specialized in finding and exposing scammers. As prevalent as romantic scamming was, there had to be organizations that could expose the scammers. Would there be a cost? She couldn't afford much, but perhaps one of those sites on YouTube that solicited subscribers would be amenable to taking on her sister's case. It was just a matter of convincing Leah to let her do it. But that was no small matter.

Brynn pulled into the space in front of her sister's trailer. Already her stomach was knotting at the job ahead of her, and an Italian dinner didn't bode well for her digestion. Maybe she'd limit herself to a bowl of minestrone soup. After turning off the engine, she closed her eyes and begged the Lord for gentle words, an unjudgmental heart, and the right response from Leah. All three things were out of Brynn's control—only God could make her idea work.

Leah appeared on the small porch and waved. A smile lit up her pretty face, the sun creating shimmers in her fire-red hair. She leaned her slight frame against the railing that swayed at the pressure, then strategically took each step down with a carefully placed foot. Her gait had stiffened, and her left leg bowed out a bit. If only there were a cure for RA—for her sister to be able to do the cheerleading stunts she used to on the front lawn. Leah had always been faster, nimbler, and stronger than Brynn and had excelled at sports. She'd even called Brynn an old lady although only two years separated them.

Brynn climbed out and opened the passenger door for her sister, who gave her a quick kiss on the cheek as she slid into the car sideways.

From the moment Brynn circled to her side of the VW bug and started the engine, Leah chattered about all the happenings with her neighbors on Burberry Lane. Most of them knew each other well. They looked out for each other—the single mothers with kids, the retired couple surviving on social security, a young couple starting out, but they relied on each other for meals, rides to the grocery store or bank, and sheer companionship. Now Leah talked about Ralph, the man from two doors down, who knocked on her door at all hours and sometimes walked right in.

"I've told him to stop, but it's like he forgets all the time."

"Why don't you lock your door?"

"Too much work. Then I'd have to get up and answer the door every time someone knocked."

Brynn always forgot, being able-bodied and all, how many times Leah actually had to count the steps to her destination. RA had done a number on her sister. "How about Licari's? I have the wheelchair in my trunk if you want to use it."

"Oh, that sounds great. I love their pizza, and I can make an extra meal out of the leftovers."

They headed east of the city. To get the conversation started, Brynn asked how Gary was doing.

"Oh, he's busy on the oil rig. I usually hear from him early in the morning. He always says the same thing. 'Good morning, love of my life. How was your breakfast?' Wonder why he always asks the same thing?"

Because he lives in Nigeria or India, and it's a safe question? "I don't know," Brynn answered.

"Yeah, and then he always asks what I ate for breakfast and if I got enough rest. It always makes me feel cared for." Her voice took on a faraway tone.

"Yeah, those are comforting questions. Could you tell me about him? After all, he's going to be my brother-in-law."

She shrugged. "What do you want to know?"

Brynn turned onto the restaurant's street. "So here's what I know about him. His name is Gary Rossi, and he's originally from Italy, but has lived in New Orleans for ten years, and he has a strong accent. He's some type of engineer. His daughter's name is Melanie, and she's twelve years old. His wife died, and when he's out on the rig, the butler watches his daughter. Is that right? Doesn't it seem odd that a butler would watch his child? I mean, who has a butler nowadays—the king and Mr. Boddy in the Clue game are the only two that come to mind."

"I think that's one of the reasons why he wants to marry me, so Melanie will have a mother."

Brynn cut a glance at her sister when they stopped at a red light. "So how do you feel about that?"

She pulled the visor down to block the late-afternoon sun. "I wouldn't mind being her stepmother, though I can't move around much. Gary says he'll hire someone to clean the house, and he has a pool in the backyard. He says he'll do whatever it takes to get me back on my feet. What I wouldn't do to walk again without this stupid cane."

Did she dare bring it up now? It would change the atmosphere. Leah would shut down, and this trip would be for naught. She'd take a baby step. "What if…what if he doesn't come? I know he didn't—"

"I know." Leah spewed the words out, her voice already becoming hard. "He didn't come at Christmas or Valentine's Day or the Fourth of July. It's because things happen. There was the burn he suffered from the furnace. The doctor wouldn't let him off the boat. That's the life of the men on the oil rig. He'll show up when he can."

Brynn didn't respond, her lips tightening. This wasn't going to end well. Maybe she should just enjoy a meal with her one and only sister, and maybe she could pursue exposing the scammer in secret.

They pulled into the parking lot of the restaurant and got as close as they could to the front door. "Ready?" She offered a smile to dilute the tension. It wouldn't go away entirely; she'd been through this before with her sister.

"Yeah, but I don't want to talk about this anymore. I just want to enjoy the meal."

"Maybe you could show me some pictures of him while we're waiting?"

"Sure." Leah pulled herself to a standing position, grabbed her cane, and held onto the side of the car until she was on the sidewalk.

Brynn wanted to cry at the thin woman with the jaunty pony tail. She was so young to have to walk with a cane. Every decision Leah made was tied to the distance to a chair or a bench. Simple things like getting the mail or walking to the bathroom were monumental tasks. And all she had was this one man who filled her with hope. Yet he wasn't real. And Brynn was sure he was taking what little money her sister had.

The waiter sat them at the closest table after Leah pointed at the one she wanted. They pored over the menus, but both already knew what they wanted. Leah ordered a medium bocce pizza because she liked salami, and Brynn stuck to the soup and a wedge salad. They sipped on frosty glasses of water and nibbled on torn-off pieces of warm bread, dipped in olive oil and herbs.

Brynn had purposely taken the seat next to her sister instead of across from her, so it would be easier to see Leah's phone. "Could you show me his pictures while we're waiting?" She tried to sound casual.

"Here are a few new ones. He sent me one of his burnt arm." Leah flicked through them, then shifted the phone so she could see a picture of a bandaged arm and nothing else.

Brynn suppressed the retort that it could be anyone's arm. "It looks like he's in a hospital or a clinic?"

"There's a doctor on the oil rig. Gary says it has a full hospital wing. They do all kinds of surgery. Here are some more pictures. One of Melanie and one of Gary by his pool. I can't wait to use that pool. It's pretty, isn't it?"

Brynn first studied the picture of a young dark-haired girl about ten or eleven. A sweet-looking girl with curious eyes, posing by an oak tree. It could have been any girl from Google images. She swallowed past the lump of bread that stuck in her throat. "Pretty girl. Have you ever talked to her?"

"Once she called me to say thank you for a gift card I sent for her birthday. She told me I made her dad very happy." Leah popped a piece of bread in her mouth. "Mm, this is so good."

"So you sent her a gift card?"

"That's what she wanted. Like most kids, she wanted to make her own decisions. It's a safe gift." Leah pointed at the picture of Gary. "He's good-looking, isn't he?"

Brynn studied the picture of a dark-haired, thirtyish man, handsome enough to be a movie star. Muscular, kind eyes, a tattoo of a snake on his forearm. "He looks like an Italian model. That pool is one those infinity ones. They cost a pretty penny." She took a sip of her soup to suppress the question on her tongue. Why was a guy that handsome and rich talking to a girl several times a day whom he'd never met?

Leah read her mind. "You're wondering why he'd ever want me when he looks like that. I've asked myself that question many times, and I've asked him as well. He says he can talk to me about anything. Gary likes the way I tell him what I think."

"That makes sense. You do speak your mind. Would you send me his picture?"

Her eyes bolted up from her plate. "Sure, but why do you want his picture?"

Here it was. She wouldn't lie. "Promise you won't get mad?"

Wary eyes focused on her. "Why?"

She took a deep breath. "I want to…check him out. If Dad or Mom were living, they'd want to meet him. You know how that goes. And now that they're gone, and I'm the older sister—the matriarch of sorts—I want to make sure he's good enough for you. In fact, I'd like to meet him. Talk to him myself. I mean, you're marrying a man I've never met. You've never met him in person. If I were in a situation like that, you'd want to know information too. "

Just then the waiter dropped off their meals and asked if they wanted extra parmesan. They both said yes. While he poured spoonfuls of the grated cheese on her soup, then on Leah's pizza, a furrow formed between Leah's eyebrows.

After he left, she toyed with her fork, swishing it across the layer of cheese. Finally she glanced up. "I guess I'm okay with you checking him out. Dad read Marty the riot act when we got engaged."

Good. "One more thing—and please, promise

you won't get mad. I just want to clear the air." She begged her with her eyes.

"Okay. What do you want to know?" She put down her fork.

"If…when Gary asks you for money, how do you send it to him?" She took a spoonful of her soup, which under any other circumstance, would delight her. But interrogation was enough to ruin one's appetite.

"Usually he asks for a steam card to pay the cost of the cellphone service from international waters or to pay the doctor fees or something like that."

She leaned her chin on her fist. "I've never heard of steam cards. Where do you buy them?"

"They're like a gift card. You can find them online or in stores like Target. But walking in Target or Walmart takes too much effort, so I just buy them online. They come in different amounts. He always says he'll pay me back when he's back on solid land." Leah picked up a crust and chewed on its end.

Brynn's shoulders immediately relaxed. Okay, that was one obstacle overcome—a small victory. They had handled a rough subject and were still on speaking terms. She was about to pursue obstacle number two—would Leah mind if she got a professional to check him out—when Leah's phone buzzed.

Leah put down her fork, picked the phone up, and read the screen. "I'll answer it later." She placed the phone on the table, screen down, and strategically cut a pizza slice into little squares. Her sister must be having a good day because usually she had trouble holding a knife and fork.

"Is it Gary?" It would be interesting to home in on their conversation; of course, it was all in the fingers. How was Leah able to text on her bad days?

"No, it's another guy I talk to. Gary never calls; he just texts."

She almost dropped her soupspoon. "You talk to another guy? While you're engaged?"

Leah mechanically chewed and swallowed before answering. "Yeah, just one other. Benjamin Fisher is his name."

"Benjamin? I've never heard you mention him before. How long have you been texting with him? Does Gary know?" Wow, she sounded like her mother.

Leah scowled. "You sound like Mom."

Brynn put her knuckles over her lips. "I just said the same thing to myself." Leah hit her in the arm when she snorted. "Sorry."

"Ben's a nice guy. He's a shrink and lives in Pennsylvania. I think he's one of those Amish people. We've been talking on the phone or texting back and forth for about eight months, but it's not every day like it is with Gary. I've told Ben everything about myself, and he always makes me feel good. And he doesn't judge me."

The words spewed out before she could stop them. "Has he ever asked you for money?"

Leah's eyes narrowed. Brynn had gone too far this time. She peered around the room for the waiter to ask for the check but didn't see him. If she stood up, that usually brought them to the table.

"Actually, he's never asked for a cent. He's really sweet and honest and sincere. Ben's like a best friend."

"Amish, huh? How did you ever meet an Amish guy online? It almost sounds like an oxymoron." She covered her mouth as another snort erupted.

"Same way I met Gary. I was playing Words with Friends on my phone. Whoever you're playing with starts chatting with you between moves. It starts with, 'Good word,' or 'You caught me there.' Then they start asking questions, like, 'Where do you live?' That kind of thing."

Brynn cut up her wedge salad. After swallowing a bite, she put her fork down. "So that's how you met both Gary and Benjamin?"

"Yeah, except Gary asked me to chat with him on another site. A lot of guys do that. Don't know why, but we mainly text. He says it's too hard to get a good connection from the oil rig."

Brynn pushed her soup bowl away. She'd had enough. "So what about the other guy?"

"Ben and I exchanged phone numbers, and sometimes we talk, and sometimes we text, but because he's busy with clients, I have to wait for him to call me." A beatific smile covered her face. "Sometimes Ben writes me poems. He says he's better with his pencil than he is with his voice. He stutters and can't find his words sometimes."

Brynn's head shook of its own volition. "I don't get it. How can you speak of marriage with one guy and carry on with another?"

Her sister's eyes rolled. "It's not hurting

anybody. I get tired of watching TV all the time. TikTok is fun, but sometimes it's nice to just talk like I used to with Tim. Remember Tim, my high-school boyfriend? We'd talk for hours every night. Don't know what we talked about, but I didn't want to end the call. If you want, I can set you up with somebody." She waggled her eyebrows.

Now Brynn rolled her eyes. "No thanks. So, send me a few pictures of both guys—pictures of their faces. I'd like to check them out. Mom and Dad would want me to. Is that all right?" Cringing, she waited for the next rebuke.

"I guess so. What are you going to do? I've seen that TV show, *Catfish*, and I don't want some strange guy showing up at my door sticking a microphone in my face."

The waiter brought the check. Brynn handed him a card without even looking at the amount. If Leah were to cause a scene, at least they were almost finished here. "Okay, don't be mad. I just want to be sure that you're getting into a good marriage. Normally, I'd have the chance to get to know him. So what I was wondering if—" She paused to summon her fledgling courage. "—I could talk to Gary and Benjamin on the phone, or if I could hire a private eye…who could quietly do a check on them to see if they're on the up and up." She hazarded a glance at her sister's face.

Her eyebrows stormed, but she was busy trying to stuff her leftover pizza into a rather small to-go container. "Go for it. I don't care. You're not going to trust me to make a wise decision, so go for it." Her lips pressed together in a single line. And the air thickened once again.

When the waiter had brought her card back, she added a tip, signed and stuffed her card in her purse. Then she helped her sister put the leftovers container in a plastic sack with the restaurant's logo on both sides. Well, at least she had Leah's permission. Brynn picked up her sister's cane and cleared the pathway of chairs ahead of her to the exit door.

Since she'd already dug herself into a hole, she might as well fall all the way in by asking how much money she'd given to Gary and Benjamin, but she'd wait until they were safe inside the car with the windows up. The catfish chasers would want to know. "If I hire a PI, he's going to want to know how much money you gave them. I promise I won't react; I just want the truth." Brynn looked straight ahead and tried to see things from her sister's point of view. To realize that the man she loved was using her would not only make her feel betrayed but also humiliated. Like she was naïve. But Leah hadn't graduated to that point yet. She was still hoping he'd marry her.

A sideways glance showed her sister shaking her head, her mouth silently playing the words on her mind, as if she couldn't believe her sister would ask such a question. Her voice was low and subdued when she finally did speak. "So this wasn't about you getting to know about my fiancé; this was about you snaking information from me by feeding me. I'm not as stupid as you think I am."

Brynn pulled over into a small parking lot next to a hardware store. "I don't think you're stupid; I think you're lonely and vulnerable. You miss Marty. Who doesn't want someone to love them? But I have to be truthful, even if it hurts. I don't think Gary or Ben are who they say they are. Have you FaceTimed either of them?"

Leah just stared out the passenger side window. "I don't know how. You know how stupid I am."

"You are not stupid. And here's a promise. If I'm wrong, and I hope I am, I'll cut my hair off. All of it, and I'll let you do it. And you can call me stupid as many times as you want. Deal?" When Leah refused to look at her, she folded her hands. "Pleeeze?"

She rolled her eyes. "You're so pathetic. And yes, I will be delighted to give you a haircut."

"Yes!" Brynn fist-pumped the air. "Guess we should get going, but before we do, did you send me the pictures?"

"I sent you two of Gary and one of Ben."

Hm. She flicked her phone on, and searched for a text from Leah. There it was. She scrolled down to the picture of Gary by the swimming pool and another one of him driving a car. A good-looking guy, physically fit. Confidence exuded from the two-dimensions. What he didn't look like was a guy needing a girlfriend.

Then her eyes landed on the third picture, and her breath whooshed out. "Is…that…Benjamin?"

"Yup, he's a looker, isn't he?"

"Looker doesn't begin to describe him. He reminds me of that guy from *Dirty Dancing*!" A chiseled jawline that merited a place on a monument. Blondish curls spilled over the collar of his short-sleeved black polo shirt. He leaned both forearms on a desk, a slight smile playing on his lips. Expressive eyes that elicited trust. "He's a psychologist?"

"Yeah, and he's really polite, and nice, and— Now you get it, huh?"

"I think I do."

Chapter Two

O, what a tangled web we weave;
When first we practice to deceive!

~ Sir Walter Scott

As soon as she arrived at her apartment in Saugatuck, Brynn turned on her laptop to start the search for a scam chaser, or whatever they were called. While she waited for the computer to warm up, she put the kettle on for a cup of tea. As she stared at the kettle, she drummed up a list of keywords to use to narrow her search. The television show, *Catfish*, could be a keyword. *Romance scammer* would be another. She'd give it an hour or so to search. What she didn't have was a lot of money or time to devote to this hunt.

Once the laptop was up and running, she typed in a few words, but each one evoked a list of suggestions and warnings to avoid being scammed, but no expert popped up on the screen to help expose the scammer. Brynn added tracker, detective, sleuth, and finder, and up popped a trail of advertisements. From the length of the list, this was not a new field. She opened up a few of them and entered her name and email address in the contact section.

A glance at the clock on top of the hutch she'd taken from her mother's house after she died read ten-thirty, evoking a yawn. Morning came much too early with the breakfast she put out every day for the motel guests.

If she dipped into her savings, she could manage paying up to two thousand to one of the detectives on the list. After all, her sister was worth it.

Just then her heart gave a start when her cell phone rang. Wasn't there an unwritten rule about no calls after ten? A glance at the screen showed an area code that was unfamiliar. Normally she would treat a strange number as a robocall and ignore it, but what if it was connected to her search for a scam tracker? "Hello?" she managed, her voice cracking.

A male voice that sounded as if it came from a tunnel answered. "Hello, Brynn Kingston? Sorry to call so late, but I noticed you clicked on my website and left a message. I'm Jess Cooper, CEO of Scam Hunters." Static blocked a few of his words. "Hello, Am I talking to the right person?"

How had this guy obtained her phone number? This was weirder than weird. "Yes, this is Brynn. I'm not sure what I'm looking for. My sister is involved with a guy who says he's from New Orleans. I'm fairly sure he's scamming her, and although she won't admit it, she's probably sent him money. Guess I want him exposed, so he'll leave my sister alone—maybe even retrieve some of her money."

"That's what we do. Now where are you located? I assume from your area code, you're in Michigan. So are we, so we could meet up with you tomorrow. Just give me your address, and we'll set up a time to start hunting down this guy."

This was going much too fast. "Wait. I have some questions. How did you find my number? What exactly do you do? And how much does it cost?"

He chuckled. "We can answer all your questions tomorrow. It looks like you live in Holland or Saugatuck judging from your area code. That's about three hours from our office. So we could be there by ten."

This was too disconcerting. "How can you tell where I live? And how did you get my phone number?"

"Google maps. And your phone number? Well, that should just tell you how good we are at our job. We'll find your sister's stalker, no problem. Oh, and chances are there are more than one stalker. We'll be there at ten." Click.

She blew out a breath. Okay, this was moving faster than she wanted, but what did she expect? Any good detective could find a place on a map. Brynn turned off her laptop, grabbed a cup of tea, and headed into her bedroom. After she snuggled underneath her blanket, her plan was to make a list of questions. Best intentions. The last thought she had as her eyes drifted shut was about that psychologist from Pennsylvania. That square jaw, eyes that bore into her soul, but how could they bore from a mere picture on her sister's phone? What was his name? Benjamin? A strong name, Joseph's youngest brother in the Bible. But how could the shrink be trusted? If he was one of those scammers, he was just a pretty face with a heart as dark as the sky outside. Preying on widows and sisters who had lost so much. Well, he wouldn't get…

Her eyes fluttered opened to splashes of sunlight filtering through the small cracks of the Venetian shades. NO! Brynn whipped aside the sheets and ran into the bathroom. No lengthy shower today, which usually served to wake her up. A glance at the clock showed twenty-five minutes until the door to the breakfast room had to be opened. There was coffee to make and porridge and scrambled eggs.

Of course she put her t-shirt on backwards. Running fingers through her snarls, she gathered the strands into a messy bun while clamoring down the stairs to the office. Vanity would have to take a backseat to urgency this morning. A glance out the window showed a family sitting around a fire pit, two children chasing each other from one Adirondack chair to another.

After unlocking the door at the end of the row of rooms, she slipped in and made quick work of putting out the breakfast offerings—cereal, Danish, yogurts, muffins. Hopefully her guests would sleep in this morning, although kids and dogs had an internal clock of their own. When all was ready, she allowed herself a cleansing breath and opened the door to a few morning people, who stood outside, surreptitiously checking their watches. "Morning. Sorry, I'm running a little late. C'mon in."

A steady stream of stragglers entered the breakfast nook, some for a cup of coffee, looking like she felt, while others came prepared with extra hands to carry the family's choices out to a picnic table on the lawn. Brynn greeted them each with a smile, a dishtowel over her shoulder to mop up the usual spills.

"Morning, Fred."

The disheveled figure didn't turn around right away, cutting her a glance from under his floppy hat. "Mornin', Miss Kingston, how are you this fine September morn?"

"A little rushed." She sidled up to him. "Try the sausage biscuits. I'd like your unbiased opinion of whether they're worth ordering again." She tonged two into the rumpled paperbag, which was already half full of food. It was the least she could do for this Vietnam vet who had lost his family decades ago. He showed up once or twice a week—from where? She had no idea.

A white truck passed the window at lightning speed. What in the world? There were kids here who crossed to reach the lawn.

Brynn ran outside, flapping her arms to flag him down. What was the driver thinking? The truck did a U-turn at the end, almost veering on two wheels, and came back toward her. She stepped out into the middle of the road. Over her dead body! It would have to stop, and then she'd give the driver a piece of her mind.

It braked mere inches in front of her. Up close,

rust marred the front bumper, and dead bugs covered the windshield to the point she could hardly see through it. The driver jumped down and stormed toward her.

"What do you think you're doing? Do you have a death wish, lady?" A dark beard covered a youthful face—not much older than a teenager, a cap covered long hair pulled back in a ponytail, and sunglasses hid angry eyes. A jean jacket hung over an ecru t-shirt. His construction boots led her to believe he was some type of worker.

Her fists posted on her hips, Brynn leaned toward him. Eye to eye, chin to chin. "What do you think you're doing, racing through an area where children cross the road?"

He met her glare. "I'm looking for the manager."

"That would be me." She pointed back. "The office is clearly behind me. You had no business…" Brynn glanced back. Oh, she'd forgotten to turn the office light on. Peering back at him, she frowned. "You aren't the scam hunter, are you?"

"Yes, I am. Jess Cooper." He thrust out his hand. "Sorry about driving so fast. I was concentrating on finding the office and forgot about the speed. So you're Brynn Kingston? Nice to meet you. Is there someplace we could talk about what you're looking for?"

A car honked from behind the truck, which was blocking the road. She moved to the curb. "Please move over to the office and park in front. I have to finish up with breakfast before we talk. Park and then join us for breakfast." She pointed at the end room that was clearly marked 'Dining room,' then hurried behind the truck to apologize.

A large black cloud emanated from the exhaust pipe, hitting her in the face. Coughing, she waved her hand in front of her eyes, then scurried to the driver's window, a middle-aged man sporting a baseball hat. He drummed his fingers, his jawline taut. "I'm sorry you couldn't move. He's leaving now. I stopped him to tell him to slow down."

"Well, I hope I don't lose my tee-time. Thank you very much."

This wasn't turning out to be the best of mornings. She dashed back to the breakfast room. A glance at her watch showed it was eight-thirty—the busiest time for breakfast. Brynn winced at the 3-star ratings the motel would receive if the fruit bowl or the coffeepots were empty. She'd worked so hard to make this old place competitive. Using money from the insurance her mom had left her, she'd gutted four of the rooms and turned them into thematic resort-type rooms. People flocked to stay in the Polynesian, the Hollywood, the Roman, or the Safari rooms, and paid twice as much to stay in them. But all but one were sitting empty this weekend.

"Mommy, I don't want cereal." A little one folded angry arms around his chest, his lip protruding. "I want waffles."

"Well, that's all that's available right now," the child's mother said, her voice as pouty as her son's.

"Sorry," Brynn said as she whizzed past. "I'll bring some more out. Stay right there, sweetie." She opened the buffet warmers that held the omelets, sausage patties, bacon, and hash browns. Most of them were almost empty. Had someone wiped her out while she was otherwise occupied? She hadn't been gone that long.

It took fifteen minutes to replenish the trays and make more coffee. She'd keep the place open an extra fifteen minutes. The scam-hunter man was sitting at the corner table with two other men. Their plates teemed with scrambled eggs and waffles. Good. That would buy her some time to clean up the room and check on things in the office. Normally she kept the office locked because she couldn't be in two places at the same time. If someone needed her, they could call her.

At nine-fifteen, she locked the door to the breakfast room and posted the 'closed' sign on it. A few guests lingered, but she'd put away the food and turned off the coffeemaker. Before she headed to the office, she stopped at the scam-hunter's table and told him to meet her at the office when they finished. Jess introduced her to his companions, Paul, the cameraman, and Skip, the producer. They sported long beards—the kind that reminded her of mountain men, but all three looked barely old enough to vote much less run a business. Somehow she'd expected them to look more—what was the word she searched for—sophisticated?

After unlocking the office that sat kitty-corner to the breakfast room, she checked messages and took the cash out of the floor safe that sat behind the registration desk, so she could make a deposit at the bank. A family entered to drop off their key, and the father wanted a printed receipt, which she gave him.

For a few minutes, the office was quiet, so Brynn was able to check her emails, prepare a deposit slip to take to the bank in Saugatuck, and counted out fifty dollars' worth of bills and change from the safe to put in the cash register. She hummed, "Crazy in Love," as she filled each slot with its denomination. Children were always coming in to buy an ice cream or candy bar, and she kept a stash of pain relievers, razors, and other personal items to sell if her guests needed them.

Fingernails thrumbed on the counter above her. The sound always irritated her. Why couldn't they just treat her like a human by saying, 'excuse me'? "Sorry, I didn't hear you come in." She bobbed up to see Mr. Cooper and his associates. "Oh, hello. Sorry, I was just filling the cash register for the day."

The man gave her a knowing smile. "You do a mean Beyonce."

Her face warmed to the blotchy stage. "Well, guess it's time to get started." She came out from behind the counter and pointed at the cluster of three seats. She picked up a pad of paper to take notes and carried her bar stool from behind the desk.

The three men fidgeted, obviously eager to move past the business part of the hunting, Somehow she felt that if she didn't take control of this meeting, she'd be spending a whole lot of money she didn't have.

"So, Mr. Cooper, as I told you on the phone, my sister has two men she's texting with. One of whom has probably taken money from her. My sister is tight-lipped and defensive about what's happened. She wants to marry one of the guys and is waiting for him to come to Grand Rapids where she lives, but something always happens—"

"Let me guess," said the apparent leader. "He's been in an accident, or there's been a fire on the oil rig. Am I on the right path?"

She nodded. "His name is Gary Rossi from New Orleans. And one of the pictures he sent Leah appeared to come from a hospital. It was a picture of a bandaged arm from a burn he suffered on the oil rig."

"But no face, right?"

"Yeah, I thought that was weird, but my sister seems to think he's telling the truth."

"She has to believe he's telling the truth, or the whole thing falls apart." He gave his friends a knowing look. "So Gary's divorced but more likely widowed. He has a child who's either in a boarding school or has a nanny. How am I doing?" He peered up, pulling his beard through his fingers.

"Close. He's widowed and has a daughter named Melanie. A butler watches her while he's on the rig. My sister actually talked to her. She called to thank Leah for sending her a gift card for her birthday." She looked up. "And I don't know how much she's sent Gary. I asked her, but she evaded the question. Leah did say that she has never sent the other guy, Benjamin Fisher, money, and she was quite adamant about it; however, with Gary, she wasn't as forthcoming."

Jess scribbled down some notes, then eyed the other two men, and a message passed among them, although Brynn couldn't tell what. She had the same feeling she'd had with the shifty-looking roofer who'd shown up after a windstorm and said without even looking at her roof that he would take care of everything. But desperate times and sheer busyness made her vulnerable.

Jess looked up with practiced eyes. "Okay, here's what we're gonna do. We'll do a reverse image search of the guy's picture to see if he's who he says is. It never is." Yes, she'd seen a few episodes of *Catfish*. It was apparently easy to steal one's picture from social-media sites.

Jess was talking and she'd missed what he said. "Could you repeat, please?"

"Sure, we'll need to talk to your sister to get the facts."

Brynn tsked. "I don't know if that will be possible. Leah avoided answering when I asked her several times, so I doubt she'd give you the information. She still thinks he's telling the truth. I can tell you what *I* know, though."

Jess heaved a frustrated sigh. "Well, how are we going to convince her to open up? We'd like to interview her on film, and then get her reaction when we return from…" He looked at his notepad. "New Orleans." When he glanced up at her shocked eyes, he rolled his. "That's what we do. We expose the guy for the fraud he is. There's no other way."

She shook her head. "This isn't going to work. I'm sorry to have wasted your time. My sister will not be exploited like this for some YouTube show. She's hurting enough." Brynn stood, walked to the office door, and opened it." Skip and Paul pushed to their feet.

"Now, hold on." Jess waved for them to sit down and began scribbling on his paper. "Okay, here's what I'm going to do. We'll spin this different. Picture it." He gazed at something on the ceiling. "The sister who can't stand by and let her baby sister be defrauded. You'll be the source of our information instead of…what was her name? Leah? We'll do an internet search, take a quick trip down to Louisiana to see if we can find the guy, and maybe arrange a phone call with him. Expose him that way. All you have to do is gather some information from your sister that will help us find him. How does that sound?"

She loosened her grip on the doorknob. "So how much does that cost?"

"Travel expenses, our services…$5000."

She fought back the gasp. "Why do you have to go to Louisiana if he's not even there? And what about the other guy she's corresponding with in Pennsylvania?"

He flipped through his notepad. "I think you mentioned that the other guy hasn't asked for any of her money. There's no interest on YouTube unless someone's lost money."

"I can't afford that much. The most I can manage is $1000."

The two guys at the table started chuckling, and she felt like an idiot. A poor idiot. A poor, senseless idiot. "Sorry for your wasted time. Guess I didn't understand what the cost would be. I could have saved you a trip." She just wished they'd leave and never come back.

"Tell you what I'm going to do. If you'd comp our hotel rooms for the length of the contract—we'd need three rooms—I could do the whole thing for $2300. It may save your sister a lot more than that."

He had a point. They all were looking at her for an immediate answer. Could she put a price tag on Leah? Her old car could make it another two years before trading it in. "Okay. But I only have two rooms available for the next week."

Jess's face lit up. "Great. We have a deal."

As she registered the two rooms at the far end of the property, she pasted on the kind of smile she donned for difficult guests who demanded their bill be torn up because of splashing noises from the pool that kept them up, or because the shower water wasn't hot enough. But inside it felt as if she were falling into a vortex with nothing to grab onto. She didn't know these guys or where they came from. "Here are your keys. Breakfast starts at six-thirty during the week, seven on the weekends and ends at nine-fifteen. How long do you think you'll be staying?"

Jess shrugged, looked at the other guys, who also shrugged. "As long it takes to bring the guy down."

"Are we talking three days or a week or—?" These were the last few weeks of the year when the rooms filled up. The income she made now helped her survive the slow months of late fall and winter.

"It's hard to say. We'll work as fast as we can. And if we find it necessary to take a trip to NOLA, you can rent out the rooms while we're gone; of course, you'll have to pay for the rooms down there." He winked at Paul.

What did that mean? The vortex was spiraling closer to her feet. Get a grip, she told herself. This was for Leah, and the sooner the guy was exposed, the better. "Just so you know, I won't pay for a trip to New Orleans." Her chin lifted. *Take that.*

Skip rolled his eyes. Paul shook his head as if she was an idiot. Jess stared at her for a long minute. "Well, it will take us longer then. Just sayin'."

Once the men were gone, and the black exhaust from their truck had dissipated, she called her sister to fill her in on what she was doing. While the phone rang, she buoyed up her resolve to stay strong despite Leah's reaction. And Brynn would not hang up until she had the information she needed to give the men. Furthermore, she'd start her own personal investigation of Benjamin Fisher.

The phone was just ready to go to voicemail when her sister picked up. "Hey, Brynn. Sorry, I was texting with Gary, waiting for him to finish telling me about his plans for the day. What's up?"

"Ironically, that's why I called. I met with a bunch of guys this morning who are going to check into Gary, just to make sure he's on the up and up." Even though her sister was an hour away, she could feel the tension increase.

Her sister started squawking as she did whenever she felt indignation.

"Don't worry. Remember I said that if Dad was here, he would make sure both Ben and Gary were good men, just like he did Marty. So let me do this. If Gary was sitting right here or was listening to this phone call, I'd ask him questions, but he's not. If he's for real, then I'll give you my blessing, but if he's not, then you have to make a decision."

She mumbled something about Brynn thinking she was stupid.

"I don't, but you lost your husband, and you're lonely, and that makes you vulnerable. Now, the men are only going to be checking on Gary, and they may have questions about him, so would it be okay if I gave them your phone number? Then you could deal with them yourself."

"I have nothing to say to them."

"Okay, well, would you give me some information about Gary and Ben? What city do they live in? How old are they? Do you have addresses or emails or phone numbers for both men?"

She huffed. "I'll see what I have. Ben's last name is Fisher."

"Great." Brynn needed to bring the tension level down a brick or two. Humor usually worked. "And if you have any more pictures of the psychologist, you can send them all day to me." That brought a laugh.

"Yeah, he's a looker, all right. So what are the men going to do?"

"They showed up in a truck this morning. A big ugly, environment-destroying truck with Michigan plates, so I think they're locals, but not from here. Duck-hunter beards and clothes. Young. And they're going to stay at the motel until they're done with the investigation, so any info you can give me will help my budget because I can't rent out those rooms if they're in them."

"I'll go through old texts and see what I can find." Leah sounded distracted, and Brynn could hear pots clanging in the background. She was probably making breakfast.

"Great. Okay, send me what you can find as soon as possible. Love you." She hung up. There was nothing she could do to hurry Leah along, so she filled the next few hours with contacting repairmen, ordering food for the next day's breakfast, and checking on the rooms. Then she headed to the laundry room to help Ursula fold towels and sheets.

"When do you go back to college?"

Those beautiful sapphire blue eyes sparkled. "Three days. Can't wait." Then she must have realized what she said. "Not that I'm looking forward to leaving this job."

Laughing, Brynn waved a dismissive hand. "I know. It must be really hard to want to give up making beds and cleaning bathrooms. And don't you have a boyfriend waiting for you at Grand Valley?"

"Yes, ma'am. He's been working as a lifeguard up north, so it's been six weeks since I saw him, but we talk on the phone." She gathered her long blond hair in a messy bun before grabbing another sheet. Brynn took the other ends and they folded it into a relatively neat square.

"Well, we'll miss you. Which reminds me—I have to hire someone to take your place. And you'll be hard to replace. I received so many positive reviews about you." Her phone blipped, which could only mean… "I have to go."

Back in her apartment, she took out a pad of paper to jot down anything she could pass on to Jess Cooper. She flipped through a few new pictures of Gary with his dog by a sports car, Gary lifting a glass of beer in a busy restaurant, and Gary in scuba-diving gear. The only information Leah had sent was an address of a post office box in Philadelphia where she'd sent two steam cards to him. Philadelphia when he lived in New Orleans?

The last picture Leah sent made her breath catch. Here was a picture of Ben standing next to a horse, a large farm in the background. He cleaned down really well. What a handsome man he was. Which begged the question. Why was he, a psychologist, meeting women online?

Well, she was about to find out. Since Jess Cooper and his cohorts weren't interested in checking into Ben's background, Brynn would do it herself. She typed his name, then the word, psychologist. Then she added Lancaster, Pennsylvania. Within seconds, the same picture appeared on the screen. The man with probing eyes that connected with hers. And there was a phone number. Did she dare? Yes she did. A glance at the clock over her kitchen sink read five-thirty. He was probably gone for the day, but she'd try anyway.

After seven rings, she was ready to hang up when an out-of-breath, deep voice said, "Hello? Dr. Fisher speaking."

Brynn stared at the phone. She'd expected a secretary to answer. "Yes…sorry I'm calling so late. My name is Brynn Kingston. I…I…well, I don't know where to start."

"That's what I'm here for, Ms. Kingston. How can I help you?" She heard a rustling as if he was preparing to write down what she said.

"Well, it's not about me; it's my sister."

"Ah, your sister. Sorry to interrupt."

"No, it really is my sister. Leah McHale. Does the name sound familiar to you, Dr. Fisher?"

He paused. "No, I don't believe so. Should it?"

She blew out a breath. Why was he dragging this out? The dirty liar. There was probably a wife and a passel of kids somewhere. "I'm calling from Michigan about my sister's relationship with you. So yes, the name should be familiar."

A slew of coughing broke out on the other end of the line, to the point she held the phone away from her ear.

"Excuse me for a minute."

She heard a drawer open, a bottle open, and a few gulps. Too bad they weren't on FaceTime. She'd give a dollar to see his face caught in the act. Hopefully, he wouldn't hang up on her.

"I'm so sorry. Now, Ms. Kingston, would you repeat what you just said? Is she a patient of mine? The name isn't familiar. Perhaps she used a pseudonym? But I don't remember any patient hailing from Michigan."

All right. He was dragging this out, but at least he hadn't hung up. "My sister, Leah, lost her husband a couple years ago in a car accident when she was in her mid-twenties. Shortly after that, Leah's company downsized and she was laid off. Both those events exacerbated her RA, and she's been disabled ever since. So, she plays games on her phone, and she met you playing Words with Friends. Says you two have been communicating for the last eight months. Hear me well, Doctor. I will not allow you to take advantage of Leah. She's vulnerable and can hardly pay her bills much less support a doctor who pretends to care for her." Her voice was rising to an angry pitch. She bit her lip before he hung up on her.

An uncomfortable pause ensued. Had he hung up? "Doctor Fisher, are you still there? What would your wife say if she knew you were carrying on like this?"

"Yes, I am. I'm at a loss for words. Believe me, I have no idea who you are talking about. If your sister called me for professional reasons, I'd certainly help, but her story isn't familiar to me in any way. Ms. Kingston, are you suggesting that I'm one of those predatory scammers? Because I'm not. That's a crime and a sin." His voice was shaking, even hitting some falsetto notes, as if he were a pre-teen. "Someone must have stolen my identity."

"Yes, that's what I'm suggesting. I saw your picture on her phone. You called her last night while we were at a restaurant. At least you haven't taken her money yet, but I'm sure it's coming. So I insist that you leave Leah alone! She's been hurt enough." She bit her lip to keep from crying.

"Listen, I am not scamming your sister. I'd lose my psychologist license if I did that." His voice rose.

She huffed. "I don't know who to trust. How can I be certain you're telling the truth?"

"You can't, but the Lord means too much to me

to pull something like that. Besides, how did you find me? Did your sister give you my number?"

Her voice lost some of its anger. She had a feeling he was telling the truth. Still. "Leah showed me your picture and told me your name. She said you were Amish and lived in Lancaster, Pennsylvania. I looked you up online…Oh, I see what you mean. If you were trying to scam her, you wouldn't be so easy to find."

"Correct. Listen, I've heard about scamming; in fact, one of my patients has been a victim of it. I'm going to a conference next weekend. How far are you from Chicago? Because I could rent a car, drive up, and meet with your sister face-to-face. Tell her I'm not the one talking to her. Sometimes I hate social media. The ease at which people can defraud others. This makes me so mad."

Was he playing her? He sounded sincere. "Just under 200 miles to my sister's, and about 150 miles to Saugatuck where I live. I doubt Leah would agree to speak to you unless I was with you. She is a mess right now. Another scammer has taken her money. I've enlisted a scam-hunter company to find the guy, but I couldn't afford them to find you, so that's why I called you myself."

"All right, I'm calling the airline to change my flight, maybe cancel it until this matter is resolved. The conference ends about noon on Sunday. Then I'll be at your place as soon as I can. In the meantime, if you could prepare your sister and accompany me to Grand Rapids to meet with Leah, I'd really appreciate it. We'll get to the bottom of this."

"It's going to hurt her. She said the guy pretending to be you was easy to talk to, and apparently they talk several times a week. Leah is so fragile since her world turned upside-down. This is going to devastate her."

"Well, I am a counselor. I can help her if she'll let me." He gasped.

"What is it?"

"I wonder if there are more victims. There must be. From what I've heard about these guys, this is their full-time job. They live in India or Nigeria, and their bosses get most of the money."

"So you're a victim as well." After they said their goodbyes, she stared out the window of her apartment that looked out on the motel's swimming pool, and behind it the various fire pits and a badminton court. Some parents were trying to play with their youngsters, but the shuttlecock was going everywhere but over the net.

Was this man—this gorgeous man—innocent, or was she being scammed as well? Did she really want to get in a car with a complete stranger? All kinds of alarm bells were going off. Maybe she should call the whole thing off before he changed his flight plans. But what if he was telling the truth? If only her father was here to tell her what to do…but he wasn't. Brynn stewed about it for a while. What if? What if she could convince Milli's husband, Brett, to meet with the doctor—size him up before she got in the car with him? It was time to pay a visit to her neighbors.

Chapter Three

"When one with honeyed words but evil mind
persuades the mob, great woes befall the state."

~ Euripides

Ben checked his calendar once more, then glanced at his watch. Just one more client, and he'd be done until he returned from the conference.

Adrian Frazier was due for their weekly appointment twenty-two minutes ago. Ben audibly sighed and grabbed his phone, knowing it was useless. Adrian wasn't going to pick up. They'd done this dance time and time again. It came with the bipolar territory. On a good day, Adrian couldn't stop talking, and often Ben had to bodily lead him to the door or they'd still be sitting in the office at midnight. But on a dark day, there'd be no chuckles or chatter or promises to plan for the dark ones. That's when Adrian would go into hiding, or wherever he went.

Ben moseyed to the window that looked out on the parking lot that sat next to his office on Old Philadelphia Pike, the main road that ran through Bird-in-Hand. A car zoomed past a horse-drawn buggy that hugged the narrow lane closest to the curb. It always brought a shudder down his spine. Yes, the horses were used to fast cars from out of state or the impatient drivers from the city, but the man inside that buggy could be Ben's father or one of his three brothers. It was better not to watch. Ben pulled down the shade. If Adrian was going to show up for his appointment, he would have been here already.

Sounds came from just outside the entryway to the office. Had he locked the door by mistake? Maybe that's why Adrian hadn't shown up. Ben hurried out of his office, past the receptionist's desk that sat empty now that Abigail was on maternity leave, past the row of empty plastic chairs that lined two walls, then opened the door. He failed to suppress the huff when he saw who it was on the other side of the door.

"Happy to see you too, br-bro." Samuel leaned his scooter next to the building, then glanced up with a lopsided grin. Moving to the threshold, he brushed off his suspendered white long-sleeved shirt that sported a few grass stains. Then he took off his hat as he stepped into the office.

"Sorry, it's not you I was huffing about. I was expecting a client. Apparently, he's a no-show." His eyes traveled down Samuel's torn-at-the-knee trousers. "Did you have a spill?"

He nodded slowly. "The car didn't even st-top. I'm okay. Mamm's not gonna b-be happy with the shirt. More fuel to keep me from coming here." Sam was right. Old-order Amish families didn't cotton to their children spending their free time, what little they had, in non-Amish environments. Even though they were brothers, Ben had gone to the dark side when he'd pursued an education past eighth grade, graduated with a doctorate, and put out a shingle.

He rested a hand on his brother's shoulder, which was an inch or two higher than his. "They need to do something. Widen the roads, or better yet, create a buggy lane. Think of all the little kids that scoot home along those one-lane roads." He shook his head. "But I'm glad you're here. Remember you'll be handling the office while I'm at the conference. I need you to make some calls to set up intake interviews. Oh, and I forgot to mention that I may be gone for an extra day or two. Can you break away from the farm Monday and Tuesday?"

"Sure. Later in the day. I've heard you enough to know how to h-handle the office." He headed into the coat closet to the left of the reception desk and grabbed a garbage bag, the broom, and a dustpan. "Why the extra days?"

Ben looked up from the instructions he'd written for his brother. "It appears someone has stolen my identity and is using it to scam a widow in Michigan. I think it's best to handle the situation in person after the conference finishes on Sunday. I'll fly back afterwards." He circled the receptionist's desk and slapped his younger brother on the back. "Of course, I'll pay you for your time. Jut answer phone calls, set up appointments, and call me if any clients need immediate help. The cell phone is in the right-hand drawer." He nodded at the desk.

"Thanks, the extra money will help. I'm saving up for a b…buggy of my own. And don't worry. I can handle things here. If…if you want, I can even give advice. I'm a good listener." He smiled.

"Did you say a buggy of your own? There wouldn't be a lady out there, would there?"

Sam's eyes crinkled. At thirty, he was past the age of marrying. By now, most thirty-year-old males had a wife and a few children. Ben and Samuel were the black sheep of the Fisher clan. "Yes, there might be." Sam demonstrated zipping his lips, indicating he'd said enough.

"Well, that would make Daed and Mamm mighty happy. But, please don't give anyone advice. I don't want to lose my license. I'll throw in some extra money for the horse."

Samuel seemed to like breaking free of the farm a few times a week. He especially enjoyed playing around with the office's computer and cell phone. As Sam emptied the trash, Ben took a seat in one of the plastic chairs that lined the wall. "How's Daed today?"

Samuel sealed the trash bag, then ran a hand through his unruly, dark blond hair. He took a seat at Abigail's desk, rubbing a knuckle over his eyes and yawned. "Daed's having another one of those days. Rheu…matism. He stayed close to home this morning."

"That means a lot more work for you. No wonder you're yawning." Poor guy. His day started way before dawn on the family farm. The cows needed milking. The alfalfa and soybeans were ready to harvest, as well as the tobacco. A knife-like stab of conscience—remorse—penetrated through the thick walls he'd built. Ben, as the oldest son, should be there to help his father. Now that the two younger ones had their own families and farms, and Ben had by choice left, Samuel was the only one remaining to help their father with the farm. "That's a lot to put on a thirty-year-old's shoulders. Is there anything I can do? Hire some extra men for the next few months?" It was the least Ben could do as the oldest.

"I'll be f…fine." Samuel turned on the office laptop, his fingertips hovering over the keyboard as if touching precious jewels. He peered up at Ben, his eyes full of wonder and eagerness.

"Well, you just tell me when it becomes too much, and I'll try to find Daed some help. I mean that. Again, I really appreciate you filling in for Abigail by doing the intakes on new patients as well as cleaning the place up. There's a list in the drawer of the people to contact. I'm not going to stick around. Do you think you could lock up after you're done with everything?"

His eyes were already focused on the screen, so Ben repeated his last question.

"Wha— No problem. Could I do the intake interviews on the phone? I talk easier than in person. Even better is sending the questionnaire to them to f-fill out." He blew out a breath, looking almost more fatigued from talking than from farming.

Poor guy. His father saw Sam's stutter as a sign of laziness. The one-roomed school we went to didn't offer the services of a speech pathologist or counselor. Just the suggestion of seeking help for his brother had sent their father into a frenzy. "We don't need outsiders' help. Don't even suggest it!" he'd said.

So Ben didn't. Although every day, what happened to Hannah, his younger sister, plagued Ben whenever he thought about her death. It's what had led him into psychology against his father's will. But by that time, he'd made his bed outside the community, but just outside the community so he could keep an eye on his mother, father, and brother. Ben loved them to death even if their stubborn grasp on tradition had been the source of many an argument throughout his life at home.

Ben headed into his office to turn off his computer, write a quick note about Adrian not showing up, and put a few files in his briefcase to go over later so he'd be prepped for the clients' appointments when he returned. A glance around the office, which was most likely someone's bedroom before it became his office, appeared to be tidy. Good. Sam would be able to leave early. With his kick-scooter bike, he'd be home before dark. Bird-in-Hand was a safe community, but the back roads to their farm were unlit, and the roads were rutted.

For some reason, Ben had the feeling that his and Samuel's working relationship was on borrowed time. Things couldn't go on the way they were. How long could an Amish man live two lives in a small community like Bird-in-Hand? Working from before dawn to the late afternoon on the farm, then coming here, almost covertly, to make some extra pocket money. His mother had overcome his Daed's reluctance and had allowed Sam to come a few afternoons a week, but they didn't know nor did they ask what Samuel did while he was here. If they found out that Sam was working on the computer, his parents would never let him come back.

Ben grabbed his briefcase and car keys and headed to the front office. His brother's thumbs were dancing over the phone's keyboard. "You're getting pretty good at typing. Daed can't find out, you know."

"I…I can type faster than I can talk. It's great." Samuel's peered up. "Don't worry. I'll close up." His eyes held a faraway look, as if he were in a distant land.

Ben resisted the urge to wrap his arms around his brother and hug him. Like most twins, Hannah and Sam were close until she'd left this world— basically withering away after the love of her life had married someone else after Rumspringa. It had been hard on Sam, as if part of him had been ripped away. Which was why Ben had, against his better judgment, agreed to his brother coming to the office. But their agreement could fall apart in a moment's time. A simple passerby from the congregation peering in the window and seeing his brother, and word would spread like a wildfire in an autumn breeze.

He slid into his car, catching a glimpse of himself in the rear-view mirror, the first since this morning when he'd shaved. His curly, dark blond hair had a mind of its own. Well, there was no one coming for a visit tonight, so his hair could wander where it wanted.

A short drive took him to the one-story brick ranch house he rented. Pulling into the driveway, he picked a few weeds that sprouted in the cracks. Barking emanated from the house, and a black snout parted the sheer curtains in the living room. Rex must have climbed up on the end table, since being a dachshund left him vertically-challenged. He'd take the little scamp for a decent walk today.

Someday, when his business took off, he'd buy a hobby farm. Have some horses, maybe a few cats. Farming was in his blood, which was more than a cliché. Ben had done it his whole life, and he missed the farm—but if he were honest, what he missed the most were the long talks with his Daed. They'd sit out in the barn chatting about life while Daed stroked the back of his old tabby, Gus. The Christmas dinners with his mother's apple and cherry and pumpkin pies. The fellowship and meals with the congregation when they met in their house. He missed all that. Now, it was a lonely existence. He'd paid a price for the choice he made. Sure, he enjoyed his new church—the musical instruments, the modern songs, the Bible studies. Of course, he avoided the single ladies whose eyes locked on his when he glanced around. Someday, but now he had his business and his family to think about. Anything else could wait its turn.

After he fed the dog, he called the office to remind his brother that he'd be bringing Rex to the farm the next morning before he drove to Harrisburg for his flight to Chicago. Since he'd been shunned almost twelve years ago, his parents couldn't be in the same room with him, so Sam was the go-between. He knew his parents loved him, but it would be Sam who met him in the long driveway to the farm tomorrow morning to lead Rex into the barn. They'd done this routine many times when Ben had to fly to conferences.

Sam always told him how much their mother loved the dog, petting him and feeding him scraps from their supper. He'd even caught their Daed throwing a ball to Rex in the early evening hours, Old Gus watching his every move.

It was hard not being able to spend time with his parents, but they left him little notes, a piece of pie, a whittled bird, and Samuel kept him in the circle with news.

As he packed his bag, thoughts about the woman's call came back, coloring the evening a dark gray. How could this be happening? Did the scammer have his personal information? Credit cards, his social security number, his bank account information? And was there more than one scammer? Or was the woman who called a scammer? Hadn't Mrs. Lieberman lost her savings when a man had called ostensibly from her bank saying there was a problem with her account? When Ben returned from this trip, the first thing he'd do was cancel his cards, change all of his passwords, and maybe even take down his website.

Chapter Four

God hath given you one face, and you make
yourself another."

~ William Shakespeare, *Hamlet*

Dark brown eyes looked back at her from
the mirror. They even had the audacity to roll.
Brynn smirked. Even her reflection judged her, but
she deserved it. If the man named Benjamin looked
a fraction like the man in the picture on the website,
it was worth putting on some mascara, which she
never used because it usually clumped and made her
eyes water.

She hummed, "The Time of My Life," from
Dirty Dancing as she added little spots of color to
her cheeks. Then did her version of the aisle walk to
the full-length mirror in her bedroom.
Unconsciously she must have chosen that song
because the guy in the picture looked decidedly like
Patrick Swayze.

Was she falling for a picture? And what if he
was married? The guy hadn't said anything on the
phone, and why would he after what she accused
him of?

On her way home from church, Benjamin had texted her to say he should arrive by four, then asked Brynn to alert her sister that he was coming to meet with her. And he asked Brynn again if she would accompany him to Grand Rapids. Which was the reason for the insanity that was happening in front of her mirror. And this was insanity—a grown thirty-two-year-old woman carrying on like a schoolgirl with a crush. Well, she'd allow herself one more act of insanity by spritzing on some Avon Haiku before leaving. She'd pocketed this bottle while cleaning out her mother's drawers, thinking she'd spray the fragrance in the air whenever she needed her mom's touch.

Milli had agreed to keep an eye on the motel while she was gone. Sundays were always dead. People left before noon to return home for work on Monday, and new guests didn't check in until later in the week.

A nearby backfire of a vehicle had Brynn running to see what was happening outside. She stepped out onto her second-floor balcony to the smell of exhaust fumes. Jess Cooper's truck had just turned into the last space in front of the two rooms where they were staying.

Milli waved to her from in front of the office where she stood with her arms posted on her hips. When it was clear that nobody was injured, she shook her head and turned to go back into the office when Brynn called her name.

"Benjamin should be here any minute. Is Brett ready to interrogate him?"

"He's right here in the office. Send him on

over, but I'm going upstairs." Milli frowned when raucous laughter came from the row's end. "You need to make them leave—I'm just saying," her Jamaican tone loud and clear.

Indeed. Hopefully, this would all be over soon. Guests had complained about the noise coming from the men's rooms. One family had demanded their money back because loud music in the middle of the night had kept their two-year-old up.

She'd gone to their room and asked them to keep the noise down, but Jess and his cohorts waved her off and maintained they were wrongly accused. If there'd been one complaint, she might have agreed, but two complaints and a family leaving early, and she was ready to send them packing—literally, especially after seeing the mess inside the room when Jess had inched open the door. What infuriated her was the fact that the only rooms she'd been able to give them were the Hollywood room and the Polynesian room—rooms she'd spent a lot of her money on.

Since she and the psychologist would be driving to Grand Rapids to meet with Leah, Brynn wouldn't have time to see if the men were complying with her admonition to turn down the volume. When she returned, she'd check on things. First things first. Brynn had wheedled a reluctant consent from her sister to bring the doctor to meet with her. It would be hard on Leah to see the face of the man she'd been talking to for months and know she'd been played. If the tables were turned, Brynn would feel the same way. Maybe between the two of them, with Leah's help, they could find out who was pretending to be the doctor.

She glanced at her watch. Three minutes. She raced down the stairs to the office. Brett greeted her with a warm hug, his salt and pepper mustache brushing against her cheek.

She gazed at this man who was like a father to her. "What are you going to ask him?"

He patted her hand. "You leave that to me. I'll know soon enough whether he's worthy to take my baby girl to Grand Rapids."

"Thank you. I owe you a pizza. Just send him out when you're done with him—if he's still alive."

"I got this."

She exited the office and bristled at the gray sky. How she wished the fall weather would cooperate for once and allow more sun to shine. Brynn didn't want the man to have a poor first impression of her state.

The sound of a car turning in made her heart race. She forced quick thoughts of reality to tamp down any expectations. The guy could be married. The guy could be a liar. He was here for the sole purpose of clearing his name with her sister. Brynn prayed for a wiser, more mature form of herself instead of this schoolgirl.

A dark gray sedan pulled up to the office, and the doppelganger of Patrick Swayze slid out, and all the maturity and wisdom she'd summoned vanished in a heartbeat.

Blue eyes the color of a June sky crinkled when she offered her hand. "I'm Brynn Kingston."

His large hand enveloped hers, a warm hand, a confident hand. The calluses surprised her. "Pleased to meet you. I'm Ben Fisher." Ben smiled with his whole face, as if he was really happy to see her. He gestured toward the yard in front of the motel. "This is a throwback to my childhood. My family didn't travel, but some of the members of our town owned motels like this one. There wasn't a day that I didn't long to swim in the pools I passed on the way to school."

She nodded. "My grandparents drove my cousin, Claudia, and me to California one summer. We'd stop at motels like this all across the country, and we always insisted they had a pool. Maybe that's why I was keen to buy this motel when the owner passed away."

"I didn't think there were places like this left. Are those firepits?"

"Yes, there are six of them. Families like to go out and sit around the fire at night. It smells great. And we have the pool and hot tub. Sometimes we show movies out at the pool if the weather's good. And there's the badminton court…" and she was rambling. Brynn tightened her lips.

He didn't seem to notice. "It's just the kind of place where I'd like to stay, not just as a place to stop along the way, but as a destination."

Just then, Milli walked out. Inwardly Brynn rolled her eyes at her mentor. Nothing got past her eyes. "Hi, Milli. I'd like you to meet Benjamin Fisher from Pennsylvania. I'll be going with him so he can talk to Leah—maybe convince her the guys she spends so much time talking to aren't who they claim to be."

Milli's face broke into a wide smile.

"Welcome, Mr. Fisher. Whatever you can do to help that sister of hers, we'll be grateful." She extended her hand. "Brett's waiting inside. Now don't you worry. I'll mind the place while you're gone." She winked not so subtly at Brynn.

"Pleased to meet you, ma'am." His magnanimous smile won Milli over—Brynn could tell by the glint in her dark eyes.

Brynn rubbed her hands together. Direct was best. "Before we leave, would you mind talking to Milli's husband, Brett?"

He frowned at first, then after a few seconds, the furrows on his forehead smoothed. "Oh, I understand. Hope I pass the test."

So did she. Five minutes later, Brett's face appeared in the window, and he gave her a thumb's up. Good. She let out the breath she'd been holding.

When Ben walked out, he didn't look annoyed or battle-weary. "What a great guy," he said. "He read me the riot act."

All right. If Brett said he was okay, she could relax. "Have you ever been to Saugatuck? I know you have to hurry back, but if there's time, I could show you the town. It's not too far from here." She grabbed her purse. "You probably want to get going." She glanced at his ring finger. Nothing, but many men didn't wear wedding bands. And what was she thinking anyway? She pointed at her car, but he insisted on driving his rental.

"You're doing me a favor, Brynn. I'm in unchartered territory here, both physically and every other way. This is the first time my identity has been stolen, as far as I know, so I appreciate you coming with me to meet with your sister." He started the engine of the nondescript sedan.

Brynn cut a sideways glance at him as they pulled out into the street. "Well, I appreciate you coming all this way. I should tell you Leah may become defensive. She's clinging to the belief that both the men she's spent the last eight months chatting with are telling the truth because that means there's hope for a future for her."

He patted the seat next to her. "I'll tread slowly. Mostly, I'll ask questions because I'm a victim as well, and the more information she can give me, the greater chance of homing in on who the scammer is. When I return home, I'm going to take down my website so this never happens again."

Brynn gestured toward the exit. "This highway will take us to Grand Rapids. Since it's Sunday, there won't be as much roadwork going on." Surprisingly, the road was devoid of cars, which surprised her. "What time do you have to catch your plane?"

"I didn't make a reservation because I wasn't sure how long this would take. Most likely, I'll stay at a hotel tonight and head back to Chicago tomorrow." His eyes took on an impish look. "You wouldn't happen to know where I could rent a room, would you?"

Brynn exaggerated an eyeroll. "I might have an extra room if you'd like. Did you bring your swimming suit? You said it was a boyhood dream of yours."

He slapped his forehead with the cuff of his hand. "No, I didn't. Maybe we could make a fire instead?"

Fire indeed. Her heart was on fire, which was an odd sensation, since logic always prevailed over fancy. But she needed to know more. "Sure. So, tell me about yourself, Doctor. My sister said you live in an Amish community. Are you—"

"Amish? Not anymore. I grew up in an Old-Order family but left the order as a young adult for reasons I won't go into."

She cut a sideways glance at him. Had she offended him by asking such a question? His lips were tight, and a vein pulsed near his jaw. "Sorry. I shouldn't have asked such a personal question. It's just that I've always been curious...fascinated by the Amish culture. I didn't mean to pry."

He patted her hand. "It's all right. We...they are used to being inspected, gawked at. Even though I'm no longer part of the community, I live close to my parents' farm. My father's getting on in years, and as the oldest, I feel responsible."

Now she was even more curious about this man sitting next to her, but her questions would have to wait. The exit to Grand Rapids loomed just a few miles ahead.

"How about you fill me on your sister, so I'll know how to proceed."

Brynn turned down the radio. "Well, Leah's my little sister by two years. She's thirty. Leah was always athletic—a good swimmer, a cheerleader. She ran track in the spring. After graduation, she married Marty, her high-school sweetheart, and worked as a secretary for a moving company. Then the bottom fell out. She and Marty were trying to start a family but were unsuccessful. Still she didn't let it get her down, and they were considering adoption when Marty was killed in a car accident during a winter storm five years ago. Although it rocked her world, she was resilient, and between her job and singing with the worship team at church, she seemed to be doing just fine."

He blew out a sympathetic breath. "Imagine being a widow at twenty-five. Does she date?"

"Well, the bottom fell out further—a perfect storm of sorts. Leah's doctor diagnosed rheumatoid arthritis soon after Marty died. It's almost as if her grief exacerbated the RA which was probably already present but dormant. She has good days and bad days, but after Covid, like so many, she didn't want to go back to work. I think the year and a half at home stiffened her up and made her into a recluse. That's when she started communicating with the scammers. They tell her she's beautiful and they love her, and it gives her hope."

"It's so sad. You're right about it being a perfect storm. Infertility, her husband's death, RA, then Covid. I can't imagine how she handled it."

Brynn's shoulders lifted of their own accord. "Through the men—the one from New Orleans named Gary Rossi and through you."

Forty minutes later, they pulled into Leah's neighborhood and turned onto Burberry Lane. Brynn pointed ahead. "Her place is at the end of the street."

When he reached her trailer, he parked in front, turned off the car, and patted her hand. "Ready for this, partner?"

Chapter Five
"It is in the ability to deceive oneself that the greatest talent is shown."

~ Anatole France

"No, I've changed my mind. I'm not up to receiving visitors." Leah's voice was muffled behind the closed door.

"C'mon, Leah." Brynn rested her cheek against the door as if it would help her case. "We drove all the way over here. It won't take very long."

"I have nothing to say to him, and I don't feel well." Sometimes her sister could be so childish. Again, she knocked, hoping she'd wear Leah down so at least they could speak face-to-face. Perhaps, she was just embarrassed at having to face the evidence that she was being scammed. Brynn lifted her gaze to Ben, who stood almost a foot taller than she. "Would you mind waiting out here for a few minutes?"

"Of course, I'll be in my car." Ben gave her a two-fingered salute before heading to his sedan.

Brynn waited until he was out of earshot, then tried again. "Leah, it's just me now. Open up."

The door inched open, then Leah pulled Brynn in, slamming the door behind her. Swollen red eyes showed that Leah wasn't having a good day. "I can't let him in here to see me like this." She swiped a knuckle under her nose. "I'm sorry, but I'm not up to talking to him."

Brynn pulled her sister into a hug, rubbing her back as she thought of the best way to handle the situation. Guilt wouldn't work. Then it came to her. "The reason Ben is here is because he's worried about someone stealing *his* identity, and you're the only one who can give him clues about the person you talked to. He's a victim. Please, Leah, he's come a long way. Ben needs you to help him."

Her face scrunched but she shook her head.

"C'mon. This is your chance to make a bad situation right."

Leah smirked. "You're pathetic. I know what you're doing. I'm not stupid. Okay, let him in, but first I have to go clean up my face. Why don't you make some coffee?"

Brynn fist-pumped the air once she was out of sight. She surveyed the room. At least, it didn't require tidying-up. The poor guy was sitting out there wondering what he had gotten into. She hurried outside and, finding him sleeping, she gently knocked on the driver's window next to his head.

He startled awake, looking around as if to figure out where he was. His eyes landed on hers, and a smile erupted. He opened the window. "What did she say?"

"I told her you were as much of a victim as she

was, and that the only way to find out who had stolen your identity was to talk to her. She's embarrassed about being taken advantage of."

"I understand." He pushed open the door and slid out, stretching his long, jeaned legs.

When Brynn returned with Ben, her sister was sitting in her recliner, her hands poised on her lap like a proper lady. She'd added some lipstick and pulled her thick red waves into an updo. This wasn't just any guest visiting her sister; this was a man, at least in her mind, that she'd been communicating with for eight months. Of course, she'd want to look her best.

No amount of words could have prepared her sister for the man standing in her threshold—a man who was a better version than his picture—if that were even possible. His eyes sparkled when they landed on Leah, and his legs ate up the small distance to reach her and shake her hand.

"Leah, I'm so sorry we have to meet under these circumstances. I'm Ben Fisher." He enveloped her small hand in his.

The calm of his mellow voice would have diffused an angry mob, Brynn thought as she observed the two of them from where she stood by the island in the kitchen. He was probably very good at his job because Leah's taut expression smoothed and her shoulders relaxed.

"Would you like some tea or coffee, a soft drink?" Leah motioned Brynn to the refrigerator.

He sat on the loveseat and waved her off. "I'm fine, thank you. I'm really hoping you can help me find the guy who's using my picture."

"You look just like your picture. Like Patrick Swayze from *The Outsiders.* Derry." A beatific smile spread across Leah's face. "But your voice is different."

He rolled his eyes. "A few people have told me that, but I've never seen any of his movies. Have 'we' talked often?" Ben encompassed 'we' in air quotes.

Leah nodded. "Yes, most of the time, you'd…he'd call me at the end of the workday, a few times a week. Sometimes, he'd text me, but most of the time, he called right when I was fixing my dinner. He always said it was relaxing to talk to me after dealing with clients all day long."

Ben crossed his long leg over the other one. "Is it too forward to ask what you talked about? I'm trying to figure out how much he knew about me."

She lifted a shoulder. "Mainly about our lives. Our childhood. Our plans for the future. He told me about growing up in an Amish family—working on the farm, milking cows, getting up at four-thirty to take care of the animals before heading out to the fields. About church, his father, who'd been sick lately, and his mother who was always busy raising a houseful of children—even twins."

Ben's eyes opened wide. "That sounds like my family. It's a little disconcerting. I wonder if it's someone I know. Your sister said that the guy you talked to didn't ask for money. Is that right?"

"No, never. I could tell him anything. He didn't judge me or make me feel like I was a loser. When Gary comes—he's my fiancé—it will be hard giving up my conversations with Ben…the other guy. I'll miss him."

Ben nodded slowly, then glanced at Brynn. She slightly shook her head. Don't go there. He must have read her signal. "What else can you tell me about the guy—Ben. Our community isn't so large. I wonder if I know him."

Her sister winced as she tried to shift into a more comfortable position. "Well, he goes to church. When he talks about God, it's almost as if he knows him personally. Like he's sitting right next to him. Can you believe that?"

Brynn couldn't constrain herself. "Leah, you know Jesus personally. You committed your life to him when you were in high school, remember?"

"Yeah, I did at summer camp, but sometimes he doesn't seem as close to me as he does to Ben. He always has a story about something God did that day that amazed him. I wish I had something like that."

Don't just wish, Leah. Make it happen. But a snappish answer from her older sister wouldn't help. Instead Brynn redirected her question to Ben. "Does he sound like anyone you know?"

He nodded. "I know a few guys who live out their faith both in the Amish community and across the street."

Both her and her sister's heads cocked at the comment. "What do you mean by 'across the street'?" they said at the same time, then laughed.

"How to explain it." His brow bunched together. "Well, for example, on one side of the street are Old Order Amish houses and farms with no electricity, no cars, and no adornments on their houses' exteriors. On my side of the street are Mennonites. We live a conservative lifestyle compared to the rest of the world, but we use computers, cars, electricity, and we attend Mennonite churches which are more inclusive than our neighbors' churches. And some of us have been shunned."

"Whoa," her sister said. "So Ben can't be Amish because he wouldn't be able to call me on a phone if he was, right?"

Leah was right. "Yeah, how could he be Amish if he couldn't have a phone? But he said he worked with his father on a farm, didn't he?"

Ben bolted to his feet and paced as best he could in the small space. "Leah, could you tell me anything else about the guy you talked to? What is his voice like?"

"Oh, he has a really sweet voice. Ben makes me laugh sometimes because of the words he chooses. It almost sounds like he's speaking a foreign language. I think it's cute. And he's self-conscious about the way he talks. He told me he stutters when he's nervous, but that's why he likes to talk to me because I don't make him nervous."

Ben rubbed his hands together. "So tell me this, what days do you talk to him, and about what time?"

Hm. From the frenetic way Ben was pacing, it was clear he knew who the scammer was. Good. He'd be able to put an end to whoever had stolen his identity and lied to her sister.

Leah was answering his question. "Usually after four a few days a week. Never on weekends, though. I always wondered why he wouldn't call on his days off."

A smirk crossed his face. "I have an idea who's calling you, Leah. If it's who I think it is, you could do worse. He's a great guy."

"Who is it?" Leah chimed in.

"I'd rather not say until I talk to him. When I return home, I'll get to the bottom of it." Ben smiled at Leah. "You've probably helped him as much as he's helped you." He walked over to Brynn and offered her a hand up. "Guess we should be going. It's getting dark, and I have a plane to catch tomorrow in Chicago."

She caught the sigh before it escaped. Really? The guy was a virtual stranger. They'd shared a short drive and a phone call. There was something homespun about Patrick Swayze. That's what she called him in her head. Curls that she wanted to twirl around her finger. A five o'clock shadow she wouldn't mind brushing against her cheek even if it caused a rash. *Rein in your thoughts, Betty Lou.* Well, anyone who could win over her sister was okay in her books.

As they climbed into his rental, they sat there for a minute before he started the car. Her stomach squawked such a humorous tune that Brynn broke out laughing. "Sorry about that. It's one of those rare days when I was so busy I forgot to eat. And it's all your fault."

Righteous indignation spilled onto his face, but a slight grin belied his words. "What? On what planet would it be my fault that kept you from eating a meal?"

"I didn't sleep last night because I couldn't stop thinking about this trip to see Leah. See? All your fault." She folded her arms across her chest, lifted her chin, and waited for a retort.

"I didn't either. Guess that's the reason for our grumpiness."

"I'm not grumpy," she huffed, then noting his impish smile, she nodded. "What I am is hungry. Is he one of the dwarves?"

"I don't think so, but Doc is, and that's me." He started the car. "Let's go get you some food. Lead on."

She clicked on her seatbelt. "It's probably a good idea to eat here in town. Saugatuck closes up early." Pulling out her phone, she slid through eateries in the area. "We're not too far from Butcher's Union. I've never been there, but it has a big picture of a hamburger on its website. Moderate prices. It's rated number three on Trip Advisor. Meat and whiskey." She glanced at him. "Do your people drink whiskey?"

A laugh spurted out. "*My people*, as you call them, don't drink whiskey. And I haven't ordered one since my rumspringa."

Her eyes cut to him. "I'm not familiar with that word. *Rumspringa*?"

"Every Amish teenager has the opportunity before being baptized and joining the church to 'sow some wild oats.' They're free to check out how the world around them lives. They can wear English clothes, date English, wear makeup, smoke and drink."

They pulled into the restaurant, but it was

closing in fifteen minutes, so they decided on McDonald's drive-through.

Between munches of her cheeseburger, she managed, "Wow, I assume many don't get baptized after getting a taste of the other side. Did you 'enjoy' your rumspringa?" When he didn't answer right away, she glanced his way, noting the way his Adam's apple bobbed a few times. Had she overstepped her bounds again? Maybe Amish questions weren't welcomed. "I'm sorry. Don't answer. I had no right to pry. We… hardly know each other, after all."

He chuckled and popped a fry in his mouth. "It's fine. We're used to it. Actually, most teens return to the fold, get baptized, and marry. As for me, I didn't stray too far during rumspringa. I found an office job at the local newspaper and couldn't get enough of the computers. Most Amish kids' last year of schooling is eighth grade. But I wanted more, so I took classes online so I could continue to help out on the farm. To please my mother, I was baptized. I tried to fit in, to be happy with working on the farm, finding a wife, and having a dozen children, but I was living a lie."

Without intending to, she covered his hand with hers. "That must have been so hard for you being pulled between loyalty to your family and what you wanted in life." She awkwardly inched her hand away. "So what did you do?" She took a sip of her soft drink and threw the rest of the meal in the bag.

The apple was bouncing again. "Well, I sat my parents down and told them I wanted to go to college. My sister had died…suicide…and I needed to make sure that never happened to anyone I loved again. Since I was a member of the congregation, the bishop had to shun me. It's rough, but my brother acts as a go-between, and I live close enough so I can be there to help my father, although we can't be in the same room together. I miss them—especially my mother. We find ways to communicate, though." His smile was strained as they pulled out of the parking lot and took the nearest exit toward Holland.

For the next hour or so, they drove in silence. Tears sprouted uninvited, and she swiped them away. She couldn't imagine not being able to spend time with her mother. Every day became precious when the cancer spread. To not have been there would have killed her. How foolish she felt as she wiped her sleeve across her eyes. He must have noticed because he squeezed her hand, and it stayed there. She swiped at her eyes. "Sorry. I can't imagine what it must be like for you."

He smiled. "My cross to bear." Ben released her hand and pointed. "Is that our exit?"

"Wow. That was fast. Yes, it is." She was almost sad that their adventure was coming to an end. "So you'll be staying the night. What time will you be leaving in the morning?"

"It all depends on finding a seat. My brother will keep an eye on my office. I don't have any appointments until Wednesday, so I'm not in any hurry." He waggled his eyebrows in her direction.

Great. She wouldn't mind him staying. "Let's stop at the office, and I'll get your key. What's your pleasure? Roman or Safari?"

"What?" He almost swerved onto the side of the road that led to the hotel. "Sorry about that."

"I figured since you were able to get through to my sister, I'd like to offer you one of my themed rooms. Although you'll have to stay close to the scam hunters, who have been a bit noisy, according to some of the guests. The entrance is right past the restaurant on the right."

"Hm. Safari sounds intriguing. Sounds like a fun night."

She couldn't stop smiling. "Perhaps you can find a YouTube show that plays jungle music to mask the noise from the next rooms."

He slowed down after he turned in. It was dark, except for the orange neon lights that lit the Starlite sign by the road, the office sign, and the recessed lights over the sidewalk. She put down her window. All was quiet, except for a group sitting around a bonfire at one of the firepits. It looked like three men and just as many women. Only a few vehicles were parked in front of rooms, which was normal for a Sunday night.

After Ben parked, she jumped out, key in hand, opened the door, and flipped on the light. She gasped, frozen in the doorway. What was this? All the furniture in the lobby was moved around, newspapers and brochures that usually sat on the counter for guests to take were strewn all over the floor. An empty pizza box sat open on the sofa. That circle of oil on the bottom of the box had better not have soaked into the couch's fabric. Who did this?

Ben stood behind her. "What's going on?"

"That's what I would like to know. Someone broke in and apparently had a party in here. There's hardly anyone staying here. Who would have—?" She whipped around to face him. "The scam hunters. They must have convinced Milli to open the door for them. But why?"

She started to pick up the papers when Ben touched her shoulder. "Take a picture first."

"Why?...Oh, good idea." Brynn pulled her phone from her pocket and snapped a few pictures then hurried to put the room back in order. With Ben's help, it only took her a few minutes, but she was spurting venom by the time she finished because a bit of oil from the pizza had soaked into the upholstery. "How I wish I could undo the agreement I had made with those guys. They're out at the bonfire. I'm going to march right out there and give them a piece of the mind I have left." She rounded the counter. "But first I'm going to give you your key. Breakfast is at seven tomorrow morning unless you need to leave before that. I can open the kitchen whenever I want." She pasted her lips into a poor excuse of a smile and handed him a key. "It's number 16. Happy safari."

"Wait." His fingers curled around her arm. "What are you going to say? They outnumber you six to one. In front of their lady friends, they won't look favorably on you scolding them. I'll go with you. Ask if you can talk to the leader guy in private."

He was right. That impetuous mouth of hers had caused her some trouble when dealing with a drunken guest or ten. Logic never worked. If Ben knew a better way, he had her attention.

Bedlam. In the flames' shadows, the women, whose shirts didn't quite meet their jeans in the middle, writhed to music coming from a phone. Jess Cooper sat in one of four Adirondacks, a beer in hand, several cans littering the ground around him. His assistants, Skip and Paul, danced much too close to the ladies. *Faust* came to mind, the opera's take on Hell.

With a glance at Ben, she approached Jess. "Could I have a word with you?"

Jess seemed surprised to see her. "Sure. Just a minute." He downed the rest of his can and added it to the pile at his feet. She expected him to stagger over, but he obviously could hold his own. With a nod at Ben, he managed a smile. "What's up? You need a report or something about our findings?" His head bobbed a little almost pulling him backwards.

"That can wait until tomorrow. What I want to know is what happened to my office?"

He exaggerated a shrug. "Why should I know about that?"

"I locked it. How did you get in?"

"Ah." A little smile spread over his face. He held up both hands, rubbing fingers against his thumb. She didn't have the slightest idea what that meant.

"You mean you used money?"

He trilled his lips as if she was a third grader. "No, I can break into any office. How do you think I catch scammers?"

She didn't want to know. "Did you need a key

or something?"

"Keys. What are they? No, we needed some establishment shots for our YouTube video. Since you weren't here, we just shot a few of the space, but I'll need to ask you some questions on record for the feed." He held up a hand before she spoke. "But not tonight."

Her tongue had been suppressed long enough. "Well, next time you break in my office, could you clean up after yourself? It's a mess."

His face scrunched up. She'd probably gone too far. "Don't you have maids to do that? That cute little maid with the Swedish name—she can clean up my room anytime she wants."

A hand circled her bicep before she could slug him. "Come along."

Pulling free from Ben's grip, she stalked back to the office. What did all this mean? That anyone could break into her office? Nobody had ever tried before, or had they? Suddenly she felt very vulnerable. She kept valuables in her safe behind the counter. Things from her mother she couldn't replace. A couple hundred dollars in cash. Her passport, birth certificate. Credit cards.

Okay. They'd left the place in a mess, but they weren't thieves, and she'd agreed, at least in principle, for them to use her property to do their investigation.

Footsteps caught up. Ben's. She slowed her pace and her breath. He didn't say anything, but she owed him an explanation. "I'm okay. No harm done. Thanks for your advice. I probably would've made an idiot of myself. Let me turn off the lights in the office, then I'll walk you to your room." She took his arm, but he didn't budge. Glancing up, their eyes met. "Oh," was all she managed to say. The office could wait. Her eyes had developed a will of their own and refused to budge as well.

Ben pulled her close, rested his arm around her shoulders, and pointed to the gazebo that sat next to the swimming pool. "A lot has happened today. We need to talk about what we're going to do next."

Next? Did he mean 'next' with her sister? Or…did he mean with her? She let him lead her to the picnic table in the gazebo. They sat on the same side, their shoulders touching. Somehow, it gave her calm—that she didn't have to handle her sister and the crew of rabble rousers by herself. She'd been handling things so long by herself that this was an epiphany—this feeling that someone else could help with the load.

His voice was low like warm molasses, comforting, easygoing. "So, we have three things to discuss. One, your sister, two, the scam hunters who seemed to be celebrating at your expense, and…us."

Us. He'd felt it too. While she wanted to pass Go to number three, she'd follow his lead, but he was talking—

"Your sister has cocooned herself in a fantasy world because it's safe. But it's not healthy since the predators she's texting are not real. We can show her the truth, but she doesn't want to see it. So here's what I suggest. Is there some way you could convince her to cancel her bank accounts and credit cards, and you take them over? I know you're very busy, but if you could take over paying her bills, you'd see what she's spending her money on."

The sigh that emitted from her lips was heavy. "She probably doesn't have many bills, so once I set her up online, it wouldn't be too much work for me. The problem will be convincing her to agree to give up control of her money. I shudder to think of her reaction. When it became clear my mother couldn't take care of herself anymore, I tried to convince Mom to move into assisted living, but she treated me as if I'd betrayed her. I don't know if I can go through that again."

His arm pulled her close; he kissed her temple. "I can't imagine how hard that must have been. Well, I'd like to share the load, so if you give me her phone number, I'll see if I can persuade her to talk to me once or twice a week. We can call it marriage counseling or grief counseling. The latter is what she needs. Grief for losing her husband. Grief for losing her ability to walk and work. The goal will be to help her take charge of her present life instead of avoiding it. What do you think?"

Grateful eyes locked on his. "You'd do that? Oh, to get my sister back." Tears sprouted unbidden. "I'm sorry. It's just I miss her so much and have felt so helpless."

He pulled her closer. Tipping her chin, his lips met hers, and a new sensation shivered down her whole body. As if she was finally anchored to the harbor that had eluded Brynn her whole life. Strength and comfort and peace and hope replaced every anxious thought. She was hungry for more and more. They stayed there, lips conjoined, until she became aware of the silence.

She pulled away. "Wow. Wow. That has to be some kind of Guinness record. Hope the rabblerousers didn't walk past us." Jess and his friends had departed, the bonfire now extinguished. A check of her watch showed twelve-thirty, so she stood. "We'd better go."

The patronizing smile on his face made her whip around. "What's so funny?" The skin on the back of her neck warmed. "What did I say?"

He took her hand and pushed to his feet. "You're funny. I think our tryst is a secret for now, but no telling what your guests witnessed. Nothing wrong with a kiss."

"You're right. Well, as we started out to do, I'll walk you to your room." She pulled him onto the sidewalk, then sidled next to him, enjoying his closeness. Why did he have to live so far away? Was this what was called a 'one night stand'?

They passed the two rooms where the scammer hunters were staying. Although the curtains were closed, a bit of light escaped from the space where they didn't meet the wall. At least no noise came from within. Tomorrow she'd meet with Jess for their findings, and hopefully, she could convince him to leave.

When they reached Ben's room, he stopped and pulled her into his arms. His voice was husky when he said, "Well, now we're in a pickle."

She knew exactly what he meant. "Do you mean this?" Her finger darted between his chest and her chin.

"Yup. Question. How do you feel about long-distance relationships?"

She looked into his smoky eyes. "I have no idea. Didn't see this coming."

"Me neither. We'll wade our way through."

Chapter Six
"No man has a good enough memory to be a
successful liar."

~ Abraham Lincoln

Her eyes opened before her alarm played
the most annoying ditty, but this morning she
sprang out of bed and hummed along with it as she
jumped in the shower and slid into a clean pair of
jeans and a new floral top. Just in case he hadn't left
early.

Brynn bustled down to the breakfast room and
filled the coffee and hot water canisters, then took
out some fresh muffins she'd picked up at the
market after church yesterday. Just in case he
showed up. Still humming, she frowned and
changed the tune to something more spiritual, then
heated the frittatas, sausage, and biscuits. Since only
six rooms were occupied, she didn't bother bringing
out too many choices of cereal. A pitcher of orange
juice, a few bananas and oranges, and she was
ready.

A glance at her watch showed she had ten
minutes before she had to unlock the door for the
guests. Ten minutes was long enough to fill the cash

register with two-hundred dollars' worth of bills and coins for the upcoming day.

With a glance back at the breakfast room to make sure she hadn't forgotten anything, Brynn hurried to the office, unlocked the door, shaking her head as the memory of last night returned, then turned on the light and slipped behind the counter. Bending down, she took the ring of keys clipped to her jeans, felt for the little key that opened the vault, and went to insert it.

It wasn't there. The vault. Her vault—the one that held her most treasured possessions, and all of the important papers she needed to run the motel. Gone.

She fell back until she was sitting on the floor behind the counter. How foolish she'd been not to listen to Milli's advice. Although the vault was the size of a mini-fridge and could only be opened with a key and the code, Milli had warned her that it wasn't safe. Someone could shoot it open.

It had to be Jess. Maybe they'd even taken it last night. She hadn't looked behind the counter. Why hadn't she? Love made her stupid, that's why. Well, this wasn't just a messed-up room; this was a crime scene. Although most of the things in the vault had no material value except to her, it also contained two-hundred dollars, her checkbook, and her credit cards. Now she'd have to cancel everything. But first she'd call the police—that's what she would do. Let them deal with the scam hunters.

Despite a few tears, she started giggling. The irony of it all. She'd been scammed by the very guys she'd paid to find the scammer.

A knock on the door made her leap to her feet. Swiping at her cheeks, she circled the counter to open the door.

Ben stood there, a tiny smirk on his face. "Ah, you're already at work."

She stepped aside and sniffed. "Good morning. C'mon in. Or rather follow me. I forgot to unlock the breakfast door." Shielding her face, she tried to sidestep him, but he blocked her passage.

"What's wrong?" the pad of his thumb traced the tear that trickled down her cheek.

"Just wait here. I'll be right back." Business first. She hurried past him before he asked more questions. Unlocking the door to the breakfast room, Brynn cast a quick glimpse around the room. Everything was as ready as it was going to be. She rushed back to the office.

Ben was standing at the counter with his key. "I just wanted to say goodbye, but first I need to hear what caused those tears."

She nodded, her lips quivering. "I've been robbed," she breathed out. "I should have checked last night. Stupid, stupid, stupid. I have to call 911."

His eyebrows drew together. "What happened?"

She blew out a tremulous breath. "My safe is missing. I should have checked last night. It didn't occur to me. All I saw was the mess. Those guys—"

"What do you mean your safe is missing?"

"I keep it under the counter. It is…was a small one. Big enough to keep my important papers, a few hundred dollars to make change when the Coke machine or the chip machine don't work." She crumpled onto the floor, her arms tightly circling her chest. "My mom's pictures. My passport and credit cards, checks. Because it was hidden behind the counter, I thought it was safe." She peered up at him. "How could they do this? And when did they do it? I guess I should have thought about that when they so easily broke in."

Ben bent over her and enveloped her body, rocking her back and forth as the tears flowed once again.

"I have nothing." Shaky fingers scratched her cheeks.

He ran his hands down the back of her head. "Don't say that. We'll get to the bottom of this. Do you want me to go talk to them?"

"No. If they stole the safe, they're criminals. They'd just deny it. Wait." She sprang to her feet and looked out the curtained window next to the door, then backed away slowly. "The truck is gone."

He caught her from behind. "Yeah, I noticed it was gone this morning. In the middle of night, the noise from the truck's muffler woke me up, but I didn't think much about it and went back to sleep. They must have left then."

She ran a fist down the side of her face to wipe off who knows what. "They probably hadn't taken the safe when we saw them, or they wouldn't have still been sitting around the fire. Most likely, they did it right before they left. Time to call the sheriff." Brynn made the call, and the operator said since she wasn't in any imminent danger, they'd send someone out as soon as possible.

Ben pulled her into a hug, and she rested her head in the cleft of his shoulder. Moments passed before she collected herself and straightened.

"Well, they'll be here soon. They'll want to see the rooms. Yuck. I can't imagine what they'll look like, but they probably cleaned out any evidence of finding them." Her eyes opened wide. "Wait." She circled to the other side of the counter and turned on the computer. While she waited for it to warm up, she took out the ledger. "I was so flustered when they showed up that I didn't do more than glance at Jess's driver's license, but I did ask for their license plate number." She ran a thumb down the ledger to their name. "Here it is. Michigan plate. At least, I have this number, but that's all I have." Brynn glanced up at his face. "Oh, you have to go, don't you? I'm sorry. You can grab some breakfast before you leave. I'm so sorry to dump this on you." She swiped at her face. "I'll be fine."

He grabbed both of her hands. "I'm not going anywhere. You're not going through this alone."

"But you have to catch a plane."

He didn't release her hands. "Would you mind if we prayed about this? Before the police arrive. God knows where the guys are. He'll lead us to them."

"Please." But inwardly, she couldn't imagine how God could retrieve her safe from three guys in a truck who were long gone by now.

"Father, we come to you for help. You know all things, so You know where the men have taken the safe. Some of the things in it are precious to Brynn because they were her mother's. I've seen You do amazing things before, far above anything I could imagine. Show us what to do next. Lead on. In Jesus' precious name, Amen."

Stunned, Brynn couldn't think of anything to add but her own Amen. This psychologist spoke to God as if they were best friends. And what did he mean when he said, 'amazing things'? Was he referring to walking on water or parting the Red Sea, or was he speaking of more personal, recent things? She'd have to ask him when all this was over, if they were still in communication. After all, he lived a thousand miles away.

He was staring at her, and she hadn't even noticed.

"What? What's wrong?"

"I was thinking. They probably only want the cash. If we can find them, we can try to get back the rest of your things. Do you remember anything else about the truck?"

She shook her head. "Just that it was dented and white, it had a lot of rust, and it was loud enough to wake up all the guests."

"May I?" He pointed to where she was standing.

Brynn moved over as he joined her behind the counter. She pointed at the floor. "This is where I kept the safe. Unless someone was looking for it, they wouldn't find it. It was too heavy to carry, but if they had a dolly, three guys could have hoisted it onto the bed of the truck."

Ben bent down and ran his hand over the streaks on the floor where it had been moved. "Hey,

I just remembered something. There was a faded decal on their bumper. Something about "Tip Up Town." Does that mean anything to you?"

She could feel her face scrunch up, as it did when she was trying to summon up a distant memory. "Yeah, it's something from up north. That's what we Michiganders call the northern part of the state where there are a lot of lakes." The computer was up and running, so she typed in the words. "Tip Up Town is in Houghton Lake. It's a festival of sorts for ice fishing the town holds every winter." She tilted her head. "It could be a clue, or they could have just been visiting during the festival."

Just then, there was a rap on the office door. Brynn circled the counter to open it. A female police officer stood there in uniform. A long dark braid trailed over the shoulder of her light blue shirt. Freckles sprinkled her nose, and large dark eyes sparkled behind a pair of glasses.

"Hi, are you Brynn Kingston? I'm Officer Whitman from the Allegan Sheriff's Department. May I enter?"

Brynn stood back "That was fast. Yes, I'm Brynn, the one who called. Come in." She glanced at Ben, who stood at the end of the counter. "This is Benjamin Fisher. He's a friend and a guest who stayed in the room next to the men whom I think took the safe."

Officer Whitman nodded at him, then took out a device that appeared to be a small version of an I-Pad. "Why don't you start at the beginning and describe what happened."

Brynn motioned toward the counter. "It's a long story." She described how she'd hired Jess Cooper, Paul, and Skip to find her sister's scammer. "They're called Scam Hunters. I don't know where they're from, but I believe they're from somewhere in northern Michigan, possibly from Houghton Lake." Brynn grabbed the ledger and read the license plate number they'd given her. She described how they'd broken into the office while she was at her sister's and how they'd taken off sometime during the night.

Officer Whitman tapped on the keys as she talked. Then she looked up. "I'll need to look in their rooms. Are you sure they're gone for good?"

"Their truck is gone. I haven't been over to check. Could you tell from the license plate number where they're from?"

"Afraid not," the officer said.

"I also have their phone number but have been reluctant to call them. Wait." She hurried to the computer and typed in the area code, then flipped through the phone numbers she'd received over the last week. "Yup, Jess Cooper's area code is 989, which is also the code for Houghton Lake and a lot of other towns in that area of the state."

Officer Whitman scrolled down on her tablet, then looked up. "Okay, so I'm assuming you didn't get their address. Did you take a look at this Jess guy's driver's license?"

Brynn cringed. She hadn't done her job. "I glanced at it, but I didn't copy down any information." She shook her head at herself. "I usually do, but the guys had me so flustered I just wanted them to leave the office."

The woman glanced up. "Flustered?"

She drew circles with the toe of her shoe, like a naughty child caught misbehaving. "I had hired them to find my sister's fiancé, but they weren't exactly what I'd expected. They were young— maybe twenty, and they reminded me of… of mountain men. You know, the kind that live off the land? Not that there's anything wrong with it." She sounded like an old *Seinfeld* episode. Another wince.

Ben intervened. "Part of the reason Brynn was flustered, as she said, was because the men wanted a lot more money than she'd anticipated. They expected her to pay for their trip to New Orleans— accommodations, food, flights—just so they could get footage of where her sister's scammer says he lives. You know, go up to the door and confront whoever lives there. It makes good TV, but it doesn't help her sister get her money back."

The officer's braid bobbed as she nodded. "I'm getting a fuller picture. Now would you take me to their rooms?"

Brynn nodded. She didn't know if she was ready to face what awaited on the other side of the door. There was always wear and tear in the rooms, especially if the family had children or pets, and she expected it. But these two rooms were special. She grabbed two key cards and activated them.

When Ben held back, she motioned for him to come. Somehow, it would be easier to ascertain the damage with him present, which made no sense at all. She handed the keys to Officer Whitman and pointed at the far end of the strip of rooms. "It's the last two. I'll be right behind you. I have to lock up the breakfast room." She motioned with her head for Ben to go with the officer. If truth be known, she needed a few moments alone to collect herself.

She headed to the adjacent building. It was obvious from its untouched appearance that no one had stopped to eat breakfast. Brynn made quick work of moving the food to the refrigerator in the attached room, and cleaned out the coffeepots and juice dispensers. As she washed down the counters, she prayed hard for God's direction. Her life was like one of those cloverleaf intersections where cars zoomed in all directions. She had so many decisions to make—about taking over her sister's finances, tracking down the guys who'd stolen her safe. Was there a way to cancel her agreement with them so they didn't take more money?

Stealing a safe and leaving in the middle of the night most likely ended the contract. She'd have to check her bank account. And then there was Ben.

Once the room was clean, Brynn headed toward the two rooms at the other end of the row of guest rooms. Not even ten o'clock, and exhaustion descended like a heavy blanket. *Buck it up, Buttercup*, the more mature Brynn told herself. *Bad things happen, but God's got this.*

Bad things certainly did happen. That was her first thought as she opened the door to the room where Jess Cooper had stayed. Disorder was too kind of a word. Energy had to be exerted to create the type of a mess she was looking at. Even the pictures frames tilted on the walls the same way they did in murder mysteries.

She walked in, afraid to touch anything. Voices came from the bathroom, but she wasn't ready to talk yet. A lampshade sat on one of the queen beds. One of the duvets covered a window, most likely to keep light from peeking in between the blackout shades. Cigarette stains pocked the nightstand. The air smelled musty. She was better off not knowing its identity. It would take more than a few housekeepers to put this room in order. Even the carpeting was stained. Did she dare go into the adjoining room where Skip and Paul stayed? Not yet. She'd need fortifications.

She headed into the bathroom where Officer Whitman was busy fitting a paper cup into an evidence bag. Ben leaned against the shower door, his arms crossed, as he asked her questions about what it was like to be in law enforcement in a tourist area.

Brynn waited for a lull in the conversation before she made her presence known. "How's it going?"

"Hey, Brynn. I'm so sorry," Ben said. "Do you think your insurance will cover the damage?"

She shrugged, her lips starting to quiver despite her best efforts to suppress them. "Have you been next door yet?"

Officer Whitman glanced up from picking something out of the trash can with tweezers. "I don't want you going in there without me, and I'm almost done here." With one more look around the small room, she took a few pictures of the sink with her cell phone then left the room.

"All right, I think I have everything I need, so you can see about getting this place cleaned up. If I were you, I'd put in a claim with your insurance company. The deductible might be lower than the cost of repairing it." When she glanced at Brynn's face, she must have realized how cutting her words were. "It might not be as bad as it looks."

They headed to the adjacent room. The officer unlocked the door and preceded them into the room, although Brynn didn't know why. Something about compromising the evidence. Well, she was thankful the officer wasn't dismissing what the men had done to the rooms, although Whitman's reason for checking out the rooms was to find clues as to where they might go next.

Fortunately, Skip and Paul's room was a lot neater and smelled better. Three levels of fast-food containers sat in a ziggurat formation next to the television. Some chili-colored splashes of food stains covered the wall above. A few soft-drink cans sat in various places.

Ben whistled at the sight. "It looks like they were playing carnival games. That's what I heard from my side of the wall."

"How could anybody do this? They're young but not teenagers. I let them stay here for almost a week for free." She plopped down on the edge of one of the beds. "How do I move past this, Doctor?"

Ben sat down next to her and wrapped his arms around her shoulder. She rested her head against his neck. He kissed the side of her head. "It's tough, especially sitting here looking at the damage."

"So what should I do?" she rephrased her

question because this whole thing seemed larger than she could handle by herself. She leaned back against his arm trying to absorb his strength.

"First of all, I'll be here as long as you need me to be. I don't want you to go through this alone." He tipped up her chin with his finger. "Is it okay with you if I stay for a few days?"

Stay forever? "Absolutely. Do you think I should call Jess Cooper?"

"Let's ask Officer Whitman. I think she stepped outside. But first, why don't you take some pictures of this?" He gestured toward the wall. "My advice is to do the next thing." He winked and moved behind her while she snapped pictures.

They stepped outside where the officer leaned against her squad car while talking on her phone.

"I'll be right back," Brynn whispered to Ben. She headed over to the firepit where the men and their lady friends had sat around last night. Perhaps they'd left some clue as to where they were going, but other than a lot of cigarette butts and beer cans, nothing else remained. It wasn't as if they'd do a DNA test to find the guys. Brynn hurried back to catch the officer before she left. Whitman was chatting with Ben. She was laughing at something he said, and a pang of something akin to jealousy, or at the very least, irritation, welled up in her.

When she reached them, she waited for an ebb in the conversation to speak. "Officer, I have a question…well, a lot of questions. First, do you think I should call Jess Cooper, and if so, what should I say if he answers?"

Whitman stared at her for a long moment. "I

doubt he'd answer, but if he did, he'll just deny everything and make up some excuse for leaving in the middle of the night."

She tsked. "All I wanted to do was help my sister. Now I've lost things from my mother that I'll never be able to replace. The room's a wreck." Drawing in a tremulous breath and feeling like an idiot, she apologized. "I just feel helpless. What are you going to do with the evidence you collected?"

The officer linked her thumbs in her pockets. "We'll take the information you gave us along with what I collected, which isn't much, and we'll see if your guests are in the system. The damage they did to your property along with the missing safe—that's larceny and criminal mischief." She opened the door of her vehicle. "We'll be in touch, Ms. Kingston. Dr. Fisher, have a safe trip back." The officer's eyes remained on him for a beat before closing the door. Well, well, well.

They stood there, suddenly awkward—at least, she was. As always, she tried to fill the silent gap with words. "You probably want to head back to Chicago. I'm grateful for you staying to help me through this all." She offered up her best smile but fell short. Honestly, she didn't know what to do next. Sometimes being independent was plain hard.

Ben was studying her. "You have the most expressive eyes. Right now, your words don't send the same message as they do."

"What do my eyes say, Dr. Fisher?"

"Well, I see troubled eyes. Eyes that beg for help. And if you'll let me, I'd like to help you solve this problem."

Her heart swelled. "But what about your work?"

"Not to worry. I'll contact my clients and work out something with them for the time being." He took her hand. "I have a confession to make. Two confessions actually." He took her hand and led her to the chairs outside his room and sat in one of them, gesturing for her to sit next to him.

Oh, no. He was married? Lord, let that not be it. She steeled herself for his answer and decided on levity. "So, *you* stole the safe?"

A snort burst out. "Wow, I didn't see that coming. Um, yeah, that's why I'm still here. For the crowned jewels."

She giggled. "I needed that. Thanks. You said you have two confessions to make?"

"All right. Here goes. I suspect that my brother, Samuel, is the one who's been talking to your sister. I won't know for sure until I talk to him, but from what your sister said, it's him. My brother has always had a speech impediment. The school we went to didn't have a speech therapist to help him. Our Daed gave him a hard time about it, which only made it worse. Perhaps if he'd received help from an expert, the problem could have been resolved early on. It's always plagued Sam and has made him self-conscious. That's why I think your sister has helped him because he could be honest with her. He's a great guy."

She leaned over and grabbed his hand. "It sounds like they've been good for each other. That takes away some of my worry—to know the guy she's talking to isn't out to scam her." She kept ahold of his hand, and he didn't pull it away. "So you'll talk to him when you return home?"

He rubbed his thumb over her hand, which sent shivers through her, a feeling she hadn't had in a long time. "So what's your other confession?"

Ben's broke into a grin. "This might come as a shock, but while I was going to college, I earned extra money for tuition by working for a parole officer. My job was to find parolees who hadn't returned for their weekly meetings with the parole officer."

"You're a man of many surprises." Brynn still didn't understand what this piece of information had to do with her. Before she could ask him another question, he continued.

"One of the tricks of the trade was slipping a tracker on the vehicle of the person I was hunting without him knowing." His eyes held a twinkle.

"Oh…so you put a tracker on Jess's truck?"

He nodded. "Last night while they were still out at the firepit. I just had a feeling things were going to get worse after we found your office in disarray. I still had a few trackers at my house, so I'd thrown one into my suitcase before I left." His eyebrows waggled. "So, I can track them with my phone. Unless they change vehicles, I suggest you and I take a trip up north, as you call it. You game?"

Her breath caught. "Why didn't you tell Officer Whitman?"

He shrugged. "I'm pretty sure she wouldn't want me interfering with the case. And—" He cringed. "It might be viewed as violating the guy's privacy rights. So what do you say? Want to take a little trip?"

Brynn leaned forward. "But what would we do once we found them? What if they have guns?"

He stood and pulled her up. "Not to worry. We'll track them down and call the local authorities. How does that sound? I did let on to Officer Whitman that I had worked for a parole officer, but that's all I said."

Excitement bubbled up within her. What was this new sensation? She was the sensible one. It was Leah who was the adventurous sister. Brynn gulped. "I'll see if Milli can take over for a day or two. It shouldn't be a problem." She took out her phone and made the call. As it turned out, Milli and Brett agreed to manage things while she was gone. Brynn didn't foresee a lot of business, since it was weeks past Labor Day. She filled Milli in on the damage to the two end rooms and the safe's disappearance.

"Do you think they're related?" Milli asked.

"I believe so, and the police officer who inspected the rooms thought the same. So for the time being, leave the two rooms until I can call our insurance agent to do an assessment." She paused, knowing what was coming.

"So are you going to visit your sister?"

Should she tell Milli? Of course, Milli was the closest thing to a mother Brynn had. She could tell her things that she had never told her mother. Milli always gave her wise, biblical advice, even if it felt like a kick in the pants sometimes. "Can I come over and talk to you face-to-face?"

"Sure, honey bear. I'll make us some lemonade with fresh mint, just the way you like it."

She paused, and there was humor in her voice when she continued. "Will you be bringing your 'friend'?" Brynn glanced at Ben and motioned toward Milli's house next door.

He waved her off. "I'll be in my room, throwing some clothes in a bag. You go ahead."

It always felt like going home when she walked up Milli's driveway. Crisp Caribbean-themed curtains blew through the open window. It would have been a good day to open the windows in all the rooms. She knocked on the door, noting the new wreath hanging on it. If Milli had one vice, it was the craft stores that lined the sidewalks of Saugatuck.

The door flew open. "Hey, friend." Milli peered around her. "Where is your young man?" Her Jamaican accent made everything sound like a song.

"He's packing."

"Oh, dear girl, he'll be back. I could tell the minute I saw him he's one you shouldn't let get away." She took her hand and pulled her into the kitchen. "Now, you come and tell me everything." Pointing at the small round table, she said, "You sit. So where are you going for the next day or two?"

"Oh, Mill. So much has happened." Should she tell her the whole truth? *Yes* whispered from somewhere inside her. She told her all about Ben and about her growing feelings for him. "So, he put a tracker on the truck while the guys were sitting around a fire pit. Apparently he was a parole officer's assistant while he was in college. So as soon as I leave here and throw some clothes in a bag, we'll be hunting the hunters."

Milli's eyes rested on her though she remained silent. Knowing eyes. Wary eyes. Brynn had a feeling she knew why. "I like him, Milli. A lot. Think he likes me too." She circled the rim of her glass. "He does the right thing, even when it's tough. That says a lot about him, doesn't it? And he loves the Lord, stays close at hand to his parents, even though they shunned him."

Milli studied her for long moments, making Brynn feel uncomfortable under her scrutiny. "Sometimes if someone seems too good to be true, they are." She folded her arms over her thin chest and leaned back. "So you be careful on the road. You've only known him for one day. I just don't want you to get hurt. Keep your phone close, and call if you have the slightest doubt about this guy, and Brett and I will beat a path to rescue you." She patted Brynn's hand, then stood and took their empty glasses to the sink. "Well, it's about time you went and packed." When Brynn stood, Milli wrapped her in a warm hug. "You just pray, and Jesus will take care of you." She kissed her temple then walked her to the door and hugged her again.

"I'll be careful, Mom. And thank you for the warning. He does seem to be too good to be true."

Chapter Seven

"A lie gets halfway around the world before the
truth gets a chance to put its pants on."
~ Winston Churchill

His call came as Brynn tugged on the zipper
of her weekender. As always she'd packed way too
much and probably not the right things anyway. She
grabbed her phone on the sixth ring. "Hi," she said
breathlessly.

"I'm parked in front of the office. You almost
ready?" His voice was so low and steady it made
her regret doubting his intentions, but Milli's advice
had her wondering if she could trust anyone.

"Yes, I'll be right down." Here the guy was
willing to help fight her battles and she was
doubting him. After a glance around her apartment,
she clamored down the stairs. At least the guys were
gone, so she didn't have to worry about them
breaking into the office again. She'd have to take
Officer Whitman's advice and purchase an alarm
system for the office. Another expense.

By the time she opened the door of Ben's rental
and climbed into the seat next to his, it felt like the

weight of all her problems was bowling over her.

"What's wrong?" he said as he turned down the volume of the radio and peered at her.

She leaned her head against the seat and closed her eyes. "It's all getting to me." Tilting her head sideways, she met his eyes. "I feel…violated." That stupid lip of hers started quivering again. "I'm sorry. I'll be fine." Pasting on a poor excuse of a smile, she turned to him. "So where are we going?"

"Back in the house if you don't feel up to this." He took her hand and lifted it to his lips, then kissed three of her knuckles that brought a smile to her face because it tickled.

"I'll be fine. It's just that I feel a little out of control right now, and I don't like it very much."

He brushed a strand of hair that had stuck to her cheek. "I understand how you feel, but hopefully God will bring a happy ending out of all this. So shall we start?"

"Where are we going?"

Ben held up his phone. "Looks like the truck is near somewhere called Prudenville. Have you ever heard of it? The truck isn't moving."

"Yeah, I know the town. My grandparents had a cottage on the north side of the lake. Grandma and I used to go up for weeks at a time during the summer, and my grandfather would come on the weekends when he wasn't working. We'd drive over to Prudenville for groceries or when Grandma needed a perm." She sighed. "I haven't thought of that town since I was a little kid. We had a motorboat, and Grandpa would let me drive it across the lake to gas it up, which was pretty far for a nine-year-old."

After Ben had entered the destination into Siri, he pulled out onto the street. "It looks like it's a bit over three hours using I-131 North. So what happened to the cottage?"

"My grandfather sold it when I was in tenth grade. Wow, I miss that place. It's probably not even there now. Since it's on the lake, developers have probably replaced it with a bigger, nicer house. Ours was a just a two-bedroom cottage. It even had a septic tank. Grandma made me wash my hair out in the lake so as not to waste water. I didn't help the environment."

He laughed. "We weren't too concerned with the environment back in the day."

"No, we weren't." She cut a sideways glance at him. "Maybe if we have time, could we go find the cottage? It may not be there, but I think I could find the property it was on because I have a general idea where it was. We didn't have an address or a phone. I just remember it was in zone 25."

He gave her a grin. "Why not? It will give me a chance to see the real Michigan. Have you ever been to Pennsylvania?"

"No, but we've had a lot of guests at the hotel from there. Pittsburgh, Reading, Philadelphia. A lot of different accents. Is it a large state?"

He shrugged as he pulled onto the highway. "I've never really thought about the state's size, but we have a lot of very large towns, and you're right about the accents. Philly people sound like New Jersey. Pittsburgh's residents sound like you." He smirked.

"I don't have an accent."

"Oh no? Say 'cod.'"

She said the word and frowned. "How do you say it?"

"The same but not with as much nasal." He winked at her. "It's cute and endearing."

Brynn folded her arms around her chest. "Hmph. I've never been told that before."

"Well, you'll have to come to Lancaster. Then you can make fun of the way we talk. And we do have accents. My parents almost sound like they're from the Netherlands."

"You're on." Inwardly, she was doing a happy dance. He wanted to see her again. Well, maybe she was jumping to conclusions. But maybe not. *Oh, dear Lord, is this the one You've chosen for me? The one who loves You first and me second?* Logical Brynn told her to settle down and not get her hopes up. They'd only known each other for a few days. Dizzy Brynn retorted, *But if he's the one, you don't need years to find out.*

All this head conversation was making her tired. She leaned her head against the window and promptly fell asleep until a gentle nudge woke her up. She straightened in her seat and looked around. "Where are we?"

He was smiling. "You have a charming little snore."

"I do not." Although she'd woken herself a few times with what could have been a snore.

"We're just two miles from the Prudenville exit. You ready?"

"I think so. What's the plan?" She pulled down

the mirror to check her hair after her fingers tangled in a snarl.

"I put the address on Siri. We'll see where she takes us." He shrugged. "It's all we can do is take the next step—whatever that is."

Tall birch trees lined both sides of the road. She opened the window a bit and inhaled the fresh air. The cottage where she'd spent so many summers with Grandma evoked that same birchy scent from the fireplace. Good memories.

"What are you doing?"

"I'm smelling the air. It's so pure." Just then she coughed and quickly closed the window.

When they stopped at a red light, he patted her hand. "Siri says we'll be there in less than five minutes. You ready?"

She could feel her face scrunch. "Actually, I don't know what to be ready for. Are we just going to go up to their door and knock? I mean, they're criminals."

"They are. Okay, Siri is telling us to turn at the next left." He put on his blinker. "We're just going to observe from afar. Then we'll figure out what to do."

They turned onto a road where the houses were set back with only a mailbox visible from the street, and in some cases, an old desk or a mattress sat next to an unpaved driveway. Overgrown trees shaded the houses from view. It was an old neighborhood that had seen better days.

When the road curved to the right, Ben started to slow down. "It's only .3 miles. The house will be on the left." She leaned back hard against the seat as if it could shield her from being seen.

They slowed to a sloth pace. "There. The driveway is more like a path and goes way back and curves behind the trees. There's a sign nailed to a tree that reads, *Private Property. Keep out.* I think I see the truck through the trees, but I can't be sure. Wish I would have brought my binoculars, but I didn't think we'd be playing detective." He glanced in the rear-view mirror. "Car's coming. I'll pull over across the street and let it pass."

A truck roared past.

She finally found her voice. "A lot of people only come up on the weekends. We could find a vacant property not too far from here and leave the car there. Then come back on foot. What do you think?"

"We need to be careful. It suffices to say they don't want us to find them, and they won't be happy to see us." He blew out a breath then drove slowly until they found a house with a for sale sign on the mailbox. Weeds ate up the rough-hewn driveway, so it was obvious the house had sat empty for a long time.

"This property is only two houses away from your scam hunters." He turned off the car and clasped her hand. "Before we leave, we pray for God's protection and wisdom."

"Good idea," she whispered. Who knew what awaited them?

They climbed out, stuffing their phones in their pockets. Brynn followed his lead, stopping at the property line of the house next to Jess Cooper's. She had no idea what they planned to do. The colorless sky didn't lend a lot of light to the situation. In fact, it added a sinister tone even though it was early afternoon. *Film noir* came to mind.

She steeled her nerves as they crossed the property next to the scammers' location. They hurried past the house—a one story ranch with peeling paint and a sagging porch. Although the curtains were drawn, a truck was parked in the driveway. Did everyone up here drive trucks? Certainly Houghton Lake where she'd spent her childhood didn't have gangsters. This was the place where men wore flowered shirts and deck shoes sometimes with socks. Not a lot of gun-toting, fedora-donned men with thick Brooklyn accents prancing around.

The image of prancing gangsters made her giggle until she remembered where she was. They'd reached the tree line abutting Jess's property, and she still had both legs. Ben held out a hand to stop her. "Let's hang out here by the trees while we get the lay of the land." He preceded her by a foot or two, the leaves that had already met their demise crunching under their feet.

A dog barked—not a yappy little whine but a baritone, big-dog kind of bark. The kind that bit. The dog must be chained up. She could hear him lunge and growl, obviously frustrated that he couldn't fully do his job of guarding the property. In her mind's eyes, she saw a sleek Doberman pinscher. Something that ran faster than she. Maybe they should return to the safety of the car. She grabbed Ben's sleeve when he shooed her to stay back.

"I see the truck. There are a few trucks in the driveway. Why don't you stay here while I go see if your safe is in the back."

She tugged on the back of his sweater. "There's a blood-thirsty dog. Don't you think we should just stay here? We can take a picture of the truck and the address. That's all we need to take to the police."

"It's tied up. I'll be fine. I can be there and back in a minute." He kissed her forehead and was gone in a flash. She took measured breaths trying to slow her racing heart, something she'd seen women in labor do in movies. Just then a gunshot shattered the silence, then another and another in quick succession. The fourth pinged off a tree mere feet from her.

Her feet whipped her body around and bade her run back to the car, but thoughts of Ben made her root in place. He could be hurt or worse. She had to go to him, drag him if need be. The leaves crunched louder than they had minutes before, and there so many of them. The acrid smell of a bullet wafted near her nose.

She dropped down and crawled past the tree line, hoping, praying that the truck would hide her from whoever had the gun. "Ben? Ben, where are you?" she whispered as loud as she could. What if the dog was not chained up? What if the owner of the dog took him off the chain? Guard dogs were always male. Mere feet from the truck, she lowered herself to the ground to look under it. No boots, no Doberman paws. "Ben? Where—"

She shrieked when a hand covered her mouth

and pulled her head back. Her heart tatted a staccato beat, and she couldn't catch her breath. "Don't say a word," a low, gruff voice whispered. She clutched at the hand that covered her mouth, but it remained firmly planted. "I can't breathe," she managed.

"Breathe through your nose," seethed the voice. Ben? He wasn't dead. She tried to flip over but he held his hand taut over her mouth. "They're still out there. Now I'm going to take my hand away. No sound. No quick movements. We're going to go slowly back to the truck."

She wanted to throw her arms around his neck for being alive, but instead she nodded. The moment he removed his hand from her face, she pushed to her knees, then to her feet and followed Ben back to the wooded area between the houses.

He turned to face her, his finger to his mouth. "They took the dog off the leash, so if we make any quick movements, he'll be on us in a flash."

"How are we going to outrun a dog?" I whispered. The sound of barking and the crunch of leaves sounded behind her.

He took a croissant from his pocket. "From your breakfast room. Follow my lead." He headed without a sound toward the house next door and climbed onto the porch. From his pocket he extracted what looked like a Swiss Army pocket knife filled with gadgets. He used one of them to open the door.

Her mouth gaped. Did everyone break into places nowadays? "What are you doing? What if someone's home? They'll kill us."

Ben gave her the look and put his finger to his

lips again. The door opened, and he slid inside, holding the door open for her to follow him in. Then he slowly closed the door. "Hello? Is anyone home?" When nobody answered, he beckoned for her to follow him into the kitchen and looked around, then opened the refrigerator. "Just some beer bottles. No one's living here right now. We can talk."

She rapped him across the ribs. "What are we doing here? Are you nuts?"

He pointed to a ripped-apart vinyl chair. "Have a seat. I checked the truck, and the safe is still in the back. That's when someone took a few shots at me. They'll probably move it inside now. But I took a picture of it and the license plate."

Just then a gunshot pierced the quiet, then another and another and a fourth. Before Brynn could stop herself, she threw her arms around his neck. "This is too much."

"It could just be some hunters. I'm more concerned about the dog," he said, his fingers resting on her arms. "That dog was a big one. It could do some damage. That's why I figured breaking in here was safer than staying out there."

"What were you going to do with the croissant?"

He rolled his eyes. "Have a tea party with the Rottweiler. I was going to throw it at her to buy us enough time to reach the car."

"Him."

"What?"

"The dog—him. Always."

One of his eyebrows snaked up as she stared at

her. "Okay, well, guess we should call the local police. We passed the Michigan State Police building on the way here." He went to the front window to peek out. "I wonder where the dog is."

Suddenly chilly, Brynn folded her arms around her chest and rubbed her arms. "You seem to be more worried about that dog than those bullets."

"Both. Once I call the police, we should head to the car because I don't want to be arrested for trespassing. Although we have a good defense— private necessity. Most states have a law that says if our lives are in danger, we can trespass to get to safety, although we'd have to go to court to prove it." He unpocketed his phone and dialed 911.

She listened while checking outside for moving bodies and dogs. The dreary, dirty-cotton sky added to the suspense of the moment. Seeing nothing, she turned to listen. Ben was having trouble making them understand what he was saying.

"They live at…just a minute…I have their address on the phone." His finger slid down, and he read the address on the tracker. "Yes, three guys. Jess Cooper, and—" He motioned to her.

"Paul and Skip—I don't know their last names," she mouthed loudly. It occurred to her at that moment that Ben would have to tell the police that he'd put a tracker on their truck. How he was going to handle that, she had no idea.

"Yes, they were staying at Brynn Kingston's hotel in Saugatuck. While she was off property, they broke in and left her registration office in a mess. They admitted breaking in and doing it. The next morning they were gone, and so was her safe."

He locked eyes with her, and from the look of them, he realized he was falling in quicksand.

"That's right. I…we followed them up here and saw that their truck was in their driveway, so I went to see if the safe was in the truck, and the bullets started flying, so I hightailed it out of there." More questions that she couldn't hear.

"Yes, I know that they were within their legal rights to protect their property, but, Officer, they have Ms. Kingston's safe. She needs it back. I'm sure they've probably already moved it, but couldn't you check on what I've told you? Tell them they can keep the money. She just wants her business and personal papers back. Some of those things can't be replaced."

She wished he'd put the phone on speaker. Now all he was saying was, "uh-huh, yes sir," but the look on his face registered defeat.

He said goodbye and stared at her. "Well, it appears small-town folks have each other's backs. When I mentioned their names, the cop said they were fishing buddies of his."

"What else did they say?" she ventured, knowing she wasn't going to like the answer.

He shrugged. "They said it was out of their jurisdiction since the safe was taken from Saugatuck, but we could file in small-claims court in that county. So basically, they're not going to help us at all." He pushed away from the counter, came over, and wrapped his arms around her. They stood there a long time, each buried in their own thoughts.

She peered up at him. "So what do we do next?

I'm not up to being mauled by a dog."

He released his hold around her. "I'm so sorry. We gave it a good shot, didn't we? Something we'll be able to tell our grandchildren."

Her eyes searched his. What did he just say? The grin on his face meant he was kidding. Oh, well. Zero for two. It would be a mite better if he didn't joke about things like that. Not when her heart was so tender. She wasn't much different than her sister, falling for every guy that gave her a second glance. "Let's go. It's freezing in this place. I forgot how cold northern Michigan gets in the fall."

With a glance around, he opened the front door and peered toward the property where Jess was staying. "If I thought I could get away with it, I'd sneak into the back of the truck and grab the stuff inside. Let them keep the safe."

She pulled him back as he opened the door. "Don't you dare. Let's just go."

He gave her a sideways glance. "Coward."

She cuffed him in the arm. "Cowardess." He took her hand and they sprinted toward the property on the right, her ears alert for the behemoth's growl, but all she heard was the crunch of leaves under their feet.

They rushed to the car, then stopped point-blank and stared at the four flat tires. Ben circled the car, moaning with each step. "If I were a vengeful man, I'd take a pickaxe to that—"

He stopped talking.

"What?" She joined him on the driver's side of the car, then covered a gasp with her hand. The back seat window was smashed in, and on the back seat of the car sat the safe. "I don't believe what I'm seeing. Why would they do this?"

Ben just stood there shaking his head. "The rental agency isn't going to like this." He looked as if he wanted to cry. "I don't even know if they cover this type of damage."

"Should we call the police back? This has to be a crime."

Ben ran his finger along a scratch that ran the length of the door. "I don't think so. Nothing we can pin on the scammers. They'd just say, 'you got your property back.' Well, let's see if there's anything left inside." He opened the door, gingerly brushing away tiny pieces of glass that flew onto the seat. "Ouch." His fingertip went to his lips. "Looks like they jimmied the door open to the safe, so you'll have to buy a new one." He reached in, then turned around to face her. "Why don't you look inside. You have a better idea what's missing."

She nodded, swallowing the lump in her throat. It was going to cost Ben a pretty penny to pay for the damage, which was basically her fault since he wouldn't have rented a car if not for her. Her hands trembled as she inched open the door.

Tears welled with each thing she pulled out. Her passport, two credit cards, her business license, a file for taxes—all were intact. She swiped strands of hair from her cheeks and delved in more deeply. Yes, her mother's journal was there along with an envelope crammed with pictures of her father and mother when they were in the early twenties. And there it was—her mother's wedding ring, These were the things that never could be replaced. *Thank you, Lord.* The money was gone, but it was only a few hundred. Money could be replaced.

She backed out of the car and joined Ben who was leaning against its hood, talking to the insurance company or the rental agency. When he ended the call, he turned to her. "Any luck?"

"Everything's there except the money. I'm so sorry about the car. Whatever it costs, I'll pay for it."

"The rental company is sending a tow truck to take it to a repair shop. They told me to find a hotel and they'd be in touch with me about a replacement car." He took her hand. "Are you okay with spending the night somewhere around the lake?" When he cut a sideways glance at her, he added, "Two rooms. I'll find us an uber if they have such a thing at Houghton Lake." He opened the trunk to take out their overnight bags.

"Wait, I left my purse in the front seat." She opened the passenger-side door and slipped into the seat. Luckily, the thieves had left her purse. Brynn rifled though it just to make sure. Then she looked up. There sitting on the console between the seats was a legal-sized envelope with her name on it. "What's this?" Slitting it open with a fingernail, she pulled out two folded pieces of paper.

A glance at the rear-view mirror showed Ben on the phone again, so she unfolded the paper. The top one was a scrawled, handwritten paragraph.

Sorry we had to hightail it away from your place. Another job needed our immediate attention. Here is the information we found on your sister's scammer. His name is Chibueze Bolaji, and he lives in Lagos, Nigeria. I printed out a picture of the dude. Hopefully your sister will know now that she's been duped. So, job done. You found your scammer.

Signed,

There was no signature. Okay, Brynn surveyed the damage. The broken safe, the stolen money, the shattered window and what looked like an oil stain on the pleather seat where the safe had sat. Four destroyed tires and two guest rooms she'd spent thousands on and would have to again.

A verse from Jeremiah 7:9 invaded the beginnings of self-pity she was heaping on herself. *The heart is deceitful above all things and beyond cure. Who can understand it?* It didn't make her feel any better. Being scammed was worse than deceit because it made her feel violated and stupid. Like she should have known better. And not only that. She had caused Ben to be hurt. Well, she'd pay for the damage to his car, even though he wouldn't accept it.

Climbing out of the car, she rounded it to where he was and waited for him to end the call. "Okay, that sounds good. We'll be there shortly." With a click, he ended the call. "We'll wait in the car for the tow truck to show up. They're going to bring a new rental for us. I called them back and told them we needed the car to be brought to us. They said it was a slow day so they'll be here within minutes. And I reserved two rooms at a hotel." For the first time, he noticed the envelope in her hand. "What is this?"

She swallowed and handed it to him, watching as he opened and read it, then he studied the guy in the picture. In her self-pity, she'd forgotten to look at it. As if it mattered. There were scammers aplenty in her own country.

"He's young. Barely fifteen or sixteen at the most. Of course, your Jess Cooper's credibility is weak at best, so we can't be sure if this is actually your sister's scammer, but at least you and your sister can have some closure now."

She sniffed and nodded. That was all she could do at the moment. He pulled her close and kissed her temple.

"Let's redeem the rest of this trip. It's been a costly one, but you did the right thing. Things can be fixed. You did this to help your sister, and perhaps this picture will help her move on."

"Or not. She's holding on to her dream with clenched fists. But you're right. Let's redeem our time up here, and tomorrow you'll be on your way home." Brynn linked arms with him. "I'll forever be grateful for what you did for me and for my sister. Words can't—"

He detached her fingers from his arms, lifted them to his lips, and kissed them. "Then don't. It's been fun." His eyes glimmered in the descending autumn sun that filtered through the birch trees. "Think about it. We dodged bullets, broke into some poor soul's house to escape a killer dog, and we accomplished what we set out to do—to retrieve your safe." He broke into "We Are the Champions," his arm pumping sideways as if it held a stein of beer.

Just then a flat-bed truck pulled into the gravel-hewn driveway. "The cavalry has arrived. As soon as we switch cars, we'll be on our way." He pushed away from the bumper and stood to the side of the driver's door as the truck screeched to a stop. Sure enough, on the back of the truck sat a shiny silver sedan.

While they ironed out the details of vehicle exchange, Brynn took in her surroundings. Leaves were already turning lovely shades of red, yellow, and orange, many of which covered the ground like crunchy carpeting. A dog—maybe Jess's dog—barked in the distance. Jess must have tied him up. She closed her eyes and breathed through her nose, the smell of smoke redolent of the fires her grandparents used to burn in the fireplace of their cottage. Ben was right. They were the champions. If it wasn't for him, she would have been a victim just like her sister.

"Time to empty this car." Ben had come up behind her, and she'd been so deep in thought she hadn't heard him. Great detective she was. Brynn took the overnight bags out of the trunk while he maneuvered the safe out of the backseat. She slung her purse over his shoulder as he carried the safe to the new car. Meanwhile, Brynn checked the car's front and back seats as well as the glovebox for anything they might have forgotten and came up with a pair of sunglasses, the car rental documents, and a pack of gum.

Soon they were backing out of the driveway. As they passed Jess's property, they slowed down. Ben glanced at her. "If I was a teenager again, I'd want to get my revenge in some way, but I'm not." He lowered the window. "Farewell, Jess Cooper. Interesting business strategy," he yelled.

She laughed. "I guess you get what you pay for. It's my fault that I didn't check them out. If I was in high school, we would have toilet-papered their house, but in their case, it probably would have sat there until they needed it."

He cut her a sideways glance. "Did you do that to people's houses?" When she nodded, he shrugged. "That never happened at Amish schools. Of course, we didn't have cars in which to get away, and everyone's parents knew each other, so we wouldn't have gotten away with it." He stopped at a red light. "How about we go find your cottage before the sun goes down?"

"Really?" Suddenly the sun was shining even if it wasn't. "Okay, I have a vague idea where it is, but this might be a goose hunt. Follow the signs to the north shore." She settled back, her eyes darting from one side of the road to the other, looking for familiar places from her childhood. On the right was the Piggly Wiggly where her grandmother and she used to shop for groceries. Next to it was the laundromat. She remembered taking wet clothes and towels out of the washer and stowing them in the basket to be hung up on clotheslines behind the cottage.

Already Ben was turning onto a smaller road that circled the lake. It surprised her how small it seemed now compared to her view of it when she was ten years old. There was the spot she and her friend, Marilee, used to walk to for ice cream cones, but it wasn't there anymore.

"Slow down. We're getting close, but it all looks so different. These large houses weren't there. Nobody had a paved driveway." She pointed to the left. "There used to be a general store there with a single pump for gas, but it's gone. So our driveway should be…right…here."

There sat her past, now painted a different color with an addition added to the back where the kitchen window used to be. The septic tank was gone along with the shed. Gone was the swing that smelled of shellac and pine and hung from the highest tree. The next door neighbor—a grouchy man named Buck—used to yell at her and Marilee when they ran through his lawn to reach the motel kids on the other side.

A slight woman in her sixties was kneeling by a small flowerbed. Maybe she was Buck's daughter. "I don't recognize that lady, but maybe she knows who owns the cottage now."

"Let's do it." He climbed out and joined her in front, and they walked over hand in hand to the woman who was now eyeing them warily.

"Hi, my name is Brynn, and this is Ben. My grandparents used to own the house next door but sold it when I was a teenager. This is my first time back. Do you know anything about who owns it?"

She stood up and took off her garden gloves. "A young couple from Detroit. They come up on the weekends. Their mother, Maud, stays up here all summer. She doesn't drive, so she should be there."

They talked a few more minutes. Brynn asked her if she was related to Buck, but she shook her head. They'd bought the property five years ago, and prior to that, it had passed through many hands.

Brynn offered her hand. "Thank you for the information. I have so many good memories of summers spent here."

The woman blew a weary breath. "It's a lot of work, but my grandkids enjoy visiting when they can."

Before they knocked on the cottage door, she led Ben to the dock and told him how she and her friend used to sit on the end, playing Yahtzee and listening to the top 40 on the boombox. "We'd swim out near those reeds, and the next-door neighbor boys taught us how to waterski right out there." She pointed further out. "So many dreams were born on this dock. I was going to be a Broadway actress, a spy in a trench coat, an ambassador to a foreign land. Kind of missed the mark." She smiled up at Ben. "Did you dream about your future when you were a kid?"

He gazed out at the ripples on the water caused by a distant fishing boat. "I was going to be a police detective, ridding the city of crime, an FBI agent, also in a trench coat. Guess that came from watching too many episodes of *Law and Order* at my friend's house. They had a TV." He took her fingers. "Ready to go pay a visit to the old woman who lives here now?"

"Sure am." They ambled back to land, careful to sidestep the holes on the dock. Whoever lived here needed to resurface it, the way her grandfather did almost every year. Approaching the front of the cottage, she couldn't resist shielding her eyes to peek in the big picture window. There was the stone fireplace on the right, the wood-planked walls that smelled like pine, but the furniture was all new. One thing for sure, the room was a lot smaller than it had been when she was a child. A hand pulled her away from the window.

"C'mon. You're going to scare the woman. She's going to think you're a peeper." He pulled her to the side door and knocked.

"Coming," came a sing-songy, tremulous voice. The door opened, revealing a white-haired woman in an apron with a picture of a Siamese cat. Arthritis bent her over, but a warm smile radiated from her face. "Who do we have here? I don't have any money."

Ben took the lead. "I'm Ben Fisher and this is Brynn Kingston. She used to spend her summers with her grandparents in this house, and she wanted to see if it was still here. Would you mind if we came in for just a few minutes?"

"Why of course. How lovely to meet two young people. My name is Maud Cameron. Come in. I've just baked some cookies. Peanut butter oatmeal." She stepped back and gestured to the living room Brynn had just peeked at from outside.

As she stepped in, she sniffed the air. Baked-goods rather than pine trees. Memories assailed her. She turned to their hostess and offered her hand. "Thank you so much for letting me see my family's cottage. I haven't been back here since I was a young teenager." She twirled slowly. "Oh, it's so much the same but smaller."

The old woman ushered them to the sofa.

"Well, you just make yourselves at home. I'll be right back. Coffee or tea or milk?" She leaned forward as if telling a secret. "I have to say my peanut-butter cookies are a mite dry, so milk might be the best choice."

"Milk, it is, please," Ben said, and Brynn nodded her agreement. The place was so small Brynn could hear and anticipate every move the woman made in the next room. When she returned, she removed the Bible from the coffee table and replaced it with a plate of cookies, two glasses of frothy milk, and cloth napkins covered with roosters.

The Bible looked as well-worn as her grandmother's had, which brought an uninvited tear to her eye. So much had happened over the last two days good and bad, and Brynn hadn't had the chance to process it all yet, so she bit her lower lip instead, which only made it quiver.

Maud took a seat in the recliner across from them, but her perceptive eyes zeroed in on Brynn. "It must be hard seeing a place that meant so much to you, in someone else's hands."

"Oh, I'm thoroughly enjoying seeing this place once again, although, you do remind me of my grandmother, whom I miss." She swallowed past the lump in her throat. "It's just I've…we've encountered a whole lot of hard things over the last two days."

The elderly woman took a sip of her milk. "I don't receive many visitors, and sometimes the only noise is the birds outside, so I'm all ears if you want to talk things over."

Brynn glanced at Ben, who nodded. "Well, it all started with my sister and a fake fiancé." The words poured out of her mouth with hardly a breath in between. "So you see both Ben and I have experienced some unfortunate events on the way to solving my sister's problem."

Reaching over, Maud picked up the Bible she'd placed on the table next to her and flipped through. "Your heart is in the right place, my dear. You care about your sister's welfare and can see things in a more objective way than she can. But you probably already know that we can't fix other people." Her eyes held a hint of humor as she turned her gaze on Ben. "Am I right, Doctor?"

"Yes, ma'am. All I can do is listen, give them homework—things to try, but it's up to my clients to do them or not. But there's prayer and the Word of God that is—"

"Sharper than a two-edged sword? You're right, it can penetrate further than our own words ever can. You know, we Americans try so hard to dodge the hard times, but when we look back, it's those times when we became better versions of ourselves."

Maud must have heard her sniff because she came over to the couch and sat next to her, pulling her close, and patting her neck. She felt like an idiot crying in front of a virtual stranger and the other person who was seeping into her heart. Brynn swallowed hard to collect herself. She wasn't usually such a baby. "I'm sorry. I don't know what's wrong with me."

Maud waved a dismissive hand. "You don't?

You've been robbed, almost been shot, fled from a dog, and now you're reliving a place from your past. Who wouldn't cry? I want to cry just listening." Ben gasped as she pulled him into a communal hug, but his eyes twinkled. She continued. "Now you two need to see what is patently obvious even to an old lady like me. It's no accident you two have come together. Am I right? Isn't God's hand in our lives awe-inspiring?"

From under the elder woman's arms, Brynn cut a sideways glimpse at Ben to catch his reaction. Great, he was looking right at her. She averted her eyes but not before catching a hint of a smile that lifted the corners of his mouth, and he winked at her. Never in a million years could she have foreseen herself and Ben in the arms of this woman who lived in her childhood cabin.

Ben sat, releasing the woman's hold on him. Brynn took opportunity and did the same, smoothing her jeans. He took the woman's hand in his. "You are a godsend, Maud Cameron. Thank you for putting everything in perspective." He stood and offered a hand to Brynn. "We should be going."

Brynn took his hand and stood, then turned to the diminutive woman. "It has been an honor to meet you. Maybe we"—she peered up at Ben— "could come and visit you sometime?"

Maud's hand went to her chest. "Oh, that would be lovely. I would love to hear how everything works out with your sister and with—" She made a little circle with her finger.

Brynn could feel her face warm, and she could just imagine what Ben was thinking. Yikes.

Ben bent over and hugged the woman. "It would be our pleasure."

Did he mean it? Or was he just being respectful? Oh, this romantic stuff hadn't evolved since middle school. It was like she was back to being a thirteen-year-old. Well, he was going home tomorrow, and that would be it. Perhaps a call or two, and the distance would become too much of an obstacle, and they'd succumb to it.

As they drove to the hotel, his arm rested over her seat as if it was the most normal thing to do. Didn't he know he was playing with her heart? The thought caused her spine to stiffen and she sat up. He glanced at her.

"Are you okay?"

She nodded. "Where are we staying?"

"A place called Lakeside Resort. It has a restaurant and a waterslide." He cut her a grin.

"Aw, too bad. I didn't bring my suit, but I'm hungry."

He took her hand. "Me too."

It was always hard for her to stay in a hotel. She couldn't help but analyze every little detail, and more often than not, her motel came up short in comparison. But for this next twelve hours, she'd force herself to analyze less and enjoy more of her last bit of time with Ben.

They enjoyed a steak dinner in the busy resort restaurant and even shared a warm apple crisp with vanilla ice cream. Afterward, they strolled back and forth at least a dozen times along the short beach that skirted the lake. They talked about their upbringing, their faith, their dreams for the future, and by the time Brynn was back in her room, she was totally smitten.

Hours later, she pounded the pillow and flipped it to the cooler side. The clock read one-thirty. Her racing thoughts prevented sleep. She tried her normal rituals: Counting to 100 in French and every other language she could think of including Pig Latin, but it didn't help. *Is this the one, Lord*? Ben was a man of principle. He took care of his parents, even if they wouldn't spend time in the same room with him. And his Patrick Swayze jawline and muscled arms made her feel like a seventh-grader.

The main thing, however—he satisfied the first qualification she'd set up for her future husband back when she was in college. He had to love God first. From what he said and how he conducted himself, she could almost say with certainty that he did. But the second? There was definitely something akin to love growing between them. The way she caught him looking at her when she was otherwise engaged. The different times he'd alluded to future times they'd be together. Or maybe she was just imagining things, or perhaps she was projecting on him the way she felt. Too bad he was a psychologist or she'd ask him.

The big issue was the distance between Lancaster, Pennsylvania, and Saugatuck. With her business firmly planted in Michigan soil, she'd be hard-pressed to move east. And with his loyalty and concern for his parents and brother, Ben wouldn't be moving her way. What would it be like to live near an Amish community? The question brought the fatigue she needed to fall asleep.

Chapter Eight
"When I consider life, 'tis all a cheat; yet fool'd
with hope,
men favor the deceit."

~ John Dryden

The minute they were back in Saugatuck, Brynn called her sister to set up a time the next morning to visit her. In spite of the fact Leah was retired, it took her time to complete her morning rituals. Brynn had learned the hard way that impromptu meetings with her sister backfired.

"Yes, Ben will be with me. He's leaving tomorrow morning, so you'll get a chance to say goodbye before he leaves. We just wanted to share what the detectives discovered." By the flat tone of Leah's voice, Brynn could tell she didn't want to hear it. She whined a bit about having to do laundry tomorrow, but she finally agreed to a ten o'clock visit.

An hour later, a knock on the door curtailed her plan to water her plants which were drooping. Her conscience got the better of her, so she picked up the rooster watering can and called out for Ben to enter. "I'm in the kitchen." Her eyes did a furtive glance around the room to make sure it wasn't too untidy. Good, she hadn't had time to mess it up yet. Everyone had a different idea of tidiness. She wondered what Ben's tidy level was. Was he fastidious or a slob like the scam hunters?

He stood in the kitchen archway, his hair now curly and wet, and he wore a white polo shirt, fresh jeans, and a wide grin. In other words, he looked mighty fine. "So this is where you live. It's as charming as its owner."

"My plants would beg to differ. They're feeling a bit abandoned, as you can see." The sight of him reminded her of her need to take a shower. Somehow she'd picked up a lot of sand. She could feel it on the back of her neck. "Would you mind if I took a quick shower? I'm a bit gritty, and I'd like to change my clothes."

"Sure, I need to make my plane reservations. I'll do that while you're washing up."

His lower lip protruded as he peered at her face, and she realized he was mimicking her. Had her lip betrayed her?

She covered her mouth with the back of her hand and murmured between her fingers, "Help yourself to a drink in the fridge. There's some lemonade, I think. By the way, my sister agreed to meet with us at her place at ten in the morning. Will that work with your schedule?"

"I'll make it work." He moseyed over to the window over the sink and looked out at the parking lot. "Hey, later can we go make a fire? I haven't done that since church camp."

"Absolutely." As she passed him to go to her

room, the scent of shampoo and aftershave wafted in her direction. Very nice. She could get used to this.

After a shower and a bit of attention to her light brown hair which had a mind of its own, she analyzed the face in front of her. It wasn't pretty, but the parts fit together well enough. When she smiled, which she didn't do enough, that's when prettiness broke out. Maybe now she had a reason to smile more. They only had a few hours left. The thought erased the grin that had reflected back at her. Was there some way to find out if there was a future for them? What could she say? Ben was a shrink, after all, so he could probably read through anything she was thinking. Maybe she should just ask. She sent a quick prayer for an opening while they sat out at the firepit, grabbed a cardigan, and joined him in the kitchen.

Upon entering, she busied herself gathering some drinks and the makings of a charcuterie platter for their outing. If this was to be their last night together, she wanted to create great memories for both of them. Then maybe he'd come back.

"I reserved a flight to Philadelphia that leaves from Chicago at seven o'clock tomorrow night, so our trip to Grand Rapids will have to be quick."

She set the picnic basket on the table. "Wish I could convince Leah to meet us earlier, but she's not good with a change in plans." A long sigh escaped as she studied the man. She was going to miss him. It was so weird how her daily life had always seemed fulfilling, but things were going to be different now.

He must have read her mind because he reached for her hand and pulled him toward him, and in a moment, she was sitting on his lap. The thought made her burst out in a nervous giggle.

"What's so funny?"

"I'm sorry. It's just I haven't been on a…Is this a date?"

"Do you want it to be?"

She tsked. "Isn't that what all therapists do? Answer a question with a question? So, do *you* want it to be, Doctor?"

"Touché." He framed her face in his hands and locked eyes with hers. "Yes, very much." He drew her close, and their lips met and remained. This is where she belonged, and she didn't want it to end. Ever. But it had to. It was best to pull away now. She backed up, took his hands, and pulled him to his feet. "Let's go make a fire," her voice coming out in a whisper.

~

As they drove to Grand Rapids, Brynn's heart was full. Last night had cemented their relationship. They had both confirmed that they had feelings for each other, but they both realized that neither of them was in a place where they could move. So they agreed to take it a day at a time and see where God took them. If He was behind this budding romance, He'd nurture it until it bloomed. Still, Brynn had those Sunday-night doldrums—the way she always felt on the night before school. The sky matched her mood—a little gray and a little subdued.

Once they parked in front of Leah's house, Ben

took her hand. "Are you ready for this?"

Nodding, she retrieved the papers the scamming detectives had left for her. "Don't expect a positive reaction. In a sense, we're crushing her dream of a future. I feel terrible doing it, but it's not based on reality."

Before they could even knock, Leah swung the door wide open. "Come in, you two. When does your flight leave? You probably don't have much time."

Of all of Leah's demeanors Brynn had anticipated, chatty wasn't one of them. Leah waved them toward the chairs in the living room, then offered them tea or coffee. When they declined, she took a seat in her armchair. "So, what did you have to tell me?"

Brynn buoyed herself for a fight. Even if she carefully chose her words, her sister was smart enough to read between them. She pulled the documents from a manila envelope and folded her hands on top. "Well, they said the man you've been talking to doesn't live in New Orleans. He lives in a town called Lagos in Nigeria. I have a picture of him here. Do you want to see it?" She waited for the tight lips, the straight back, but they didn't come.

"Yeah, let me have a gander. Isn't that what Mom used to say?" She giggled. Who was this woman impersonating her sister? Leah reached over, peered at the picture, then sighed and shook her head. "That explains a lot of things that didn't make sense. Like when I asked him if his property had been damaged by Hurricane Laura, he didn't seem to know what I was talking about."

Brynn studied her sister. Not in a million years would she have expected such an accepting response. "So you're over Gary?"

She swiftly nodded. "When he told me his ship was almost to Michigan, but they were stuck out to sea in Kentucky, even I know Kentucky's landlocked. So I told him so, and he threw a little fit, and he blocked me." Leah shrugged. "Well, Gary kept me entertained and made me feel good about myself, so it wasn't a complete loss."

Ben sat forward, his elbows on his knees. "You don't seem to be too upset about things."

Again she shrugged. "I'm moving on. And the other Amish guy and I have been talking several times a day. It's going really good. He's made it easy for me to get over Gary or whatever his name is."

"So are you talking about the guy named Ben?"

She nodded. "I told him I had met you, and that he was lying about who he really was."

"How did he respond?"

"He didn't say much; he just became all quiet like, and I knew I had upset him. So I told him it didn't matter what his name was or what he looked like; I enjoyed talking to him."

Brynn expected Ben to respond, but he didn't. Yet the nerve ticking on the side of his neck told her he was holding back for some reason. When silence filled the room for more than a comfortable moment, she patted Ben's hand. "I guess we should be going. Ben needs to drive to Chicago to catch his flight."

He stood, crossed the small distance to where

Leah sat, leaned over, and hugged her. "You don't need to walk us to the door. It was a pleasure to meet you, and I hope we'll see you again soon."

Leah's eyes locked on Brynn's. Ben's parting words using 'we,' had caught Leah's attention, the tacit message ringing loud and clear. Now it was Brynn's turn to shrug back because she didn't have any news to tell her.

The drive back home was way too quiet, each of them enveloped in their own thoughts. His final words to Leah, that 'we'll see you again soon' had to suffice for now. But maybe Brynn was reading too much into them. It could be the queen's use of we—'We are not amused,' or 'We don't slurp our tea.' Chances were Ben was not trying to be a queen, but more likely he was just being the nice guy he was. A girl could fall for a guy like that, except she couldn't imagine being married to a guy who could see into her very soul and analyze her every word and mannerism. Married? She'd only known Ben for a few days and she was already thinking about the M word.

His voice broke through her thoughts, but not quickly enough. She cut him a sideways glance. "What did you say?"

"Sorry, I was trying to explain why I didn't react to your sister's comment about Ben—or my brother, Samuel. As I told you, I believe it's my brother. Before I say anything to her, I want to have a chat with him. The guy not only used my phone and laptop in my office, but he also used my identity. Sam's a great guy, but he's as innocent as a lamb. He's the guy that stuck his tongue on a lamppost during winter, and we had to use hot water to get him loose. He's a guy who believes the best about people, even the ones who make fun of his stuttering. Samuel probably has never heard of romance scamming before. He just wanted someone to talk to outside of our community, and more importantly, someone who didn't know him."

"So how are you going to handle this?" It was so sad for both Leah and Samuel—two lost souls who had connected on a deeper level than physical, both reaching out to each other because they couldn't find acceptance in their own worlds.

He tapped the steering wheel. "First, I'm going to confront him with what I know and ask him to admit the truth. Then we'll talk about some of the potential problems that could have occurred because of his deceit. He'll understand. In many ways, he's an old soul, and he's searching for his other half."

Her head tilted toward him. "What do you mean by, 'his other half'?"

He circled his neck to get the kinks out. "Ouch, I'm as stiff as a board. I believe God has one particular person in mind for each of us. Like a jigsaw puzzle, only one piece will fit." His eyes slid to lock with hers for just a moment, but that one glance answered all of her questions.

Chapter Nine
"The truth of the innocent is the liar's most useful tool."
~ Stephen King

After ten hours of sleep, Ben parked at the end of his parents' gravel driveway that forked one way toward the farmhouse he'd grown up in and the other way toward the two barns. How he wished his father or mother would come out to greet him with a hug, but that was a pipe dream. Instead, he beeped once to alert his brother he was out here to pick up his dog.

From the back of the house, Samuel appeared and waved in his direction. "Hey, bro," he yelled. Rex waddled behind him, and as Ben called his name, the dachshund's waddle turned into a quicker waddle, as he came toward him. Ben met him halfway and knelt to envelop him in a hug. "Hey there, Rex. I missed you so much. Sorry I was gone so long." The dog's wet tongue lapped at his cheeks.

When his brother caught up, Ben stood and hugged him. "I'm sorry it took so long. Are Mamm and Daed mad that I left Rex here so long?"

He chuckled. "Not a b-bit. They won't admit it

but they love this little guy as much as they love that old cat, Gus, especially Mamm." Samuel stepped back. "You l-look different. What's going on?"

Ben studied his brother for a minute. "We—you and I—have some things to talk about."

Samuel's gaze went to the dog, but he nodded. "I g-guess you met Leah?"

"I did. She's a nice young woman, who's lost what little money she had to a romance scammer. Leah said she's enjoyed talking to you." He paused. Was this the right time? Answer, as good as any. "Why did you do it?"

Tears filled Samuel's eyes. He brushed them away with the sleeve of his jacket. "Because I love her." His lower lip trembled.

Rarely had he seen his brother cry. It was *verboten* by their father. Ben circled his brother's neck and brought him into a hug. He held him as his shoulders racked with sobs and finally ebbed. "It's okay," he whispered and stepped back.

Samuel brushed at his face. "I d-didn't mean to lie to her or to you. It's just that I wanted to impress her, and I didn't think a farmhand would." His head couldn't have hung any lower. "F-forgive me." He didn't meet his eyes at first, then he slowly lifted them.

"Of course, I forgive you, but you cannot use my identity anymore. I could have been sued or worse, lost my license to practice. Are there other girls? Tell me the truth."

He backed up. "What? Of course not. Leah is the only one I've ever t-talked to. That's the truth."

Ben patted his arm. "That's good. Then no harm, no foul. I guess I'm partly to blame."

"What do you mean?"

"Well, I've put you in a position where you're using my phone and my computer. If Mamm or Daed knew, they wouldn't be happy with either one of us, and they'd probably forbid you to come anymore." When Rex started for the street, Ben hurried to catch him, then picked him up and put him in the car.

"But I-I don't know how I can stop talking to Leah. I've never felt this way about a girl before. It's l-like we're made for each other. I want to protect her, take care of her, but if she ever saw me—"

As Ben was lowering his car windows, Samuel's last words had him clamoring out of the car. "Sam, what are you saying?" His brother's hands were stuffed in his pockets, his head studying the ground.

He shrugged. "Look at me. What do I have to offer her? I'm not educated like you. I'm st-stuck here living with my parents, I can't say a sentence without stuttering, and I don't even know how to drive a c-car."

Ben covered the distance between them, lifted his brother's chin with a finger, and forced him to look at him. "Samuel Caleb Fisher, you are keeping our parents' farm from going under. You know how to birth a foal, repair a buggy, plant a crop and see it come to harvest. Without your help, Mamm and Daed would have lost this whole property. Yeah, one of our brothers might have bought it, but they would have hired others to take care of it. Have you ever noticed the great detail you put into everything you do? Sam, you are one of a kind." He laughed. "Look at the two of us, eyes tearing up, sniffling like we have colds."

With a nod, Sam swiped his face with a sleeve. "But w-what am I going to do about Leah? She knows the truth now. It doesn't seem to bother her that I lied to her. G-guess she's used to it. She says she likes talking to me. Says I'm a good listener, and I don't j-judge her." He glanced up. "You've seen her. What's she like?"

The longing was evident in his eyes. Ben slapped at a fly that had alighted on his neck. "It's growing hot out here. How about we climb in my car and go get an ice cream?" He roped his arm around his brother's shoulders. "C'mon, I owe you money for handling the office and watching Rex. Will an ice cream cone suffice for payment?"

With a sideways glance, Sam tsked. "Not even close." They climbed in the car after Ben scooted the dog into the backseat, then turned on the air conditioning, knowing his brother didn't get it very much. Backing up to the street, he headed toward Old Philadelphia Pike to the Bird-in-Hand Bakery, which was not too far from his office. Maybe he could convince Sam to show him what had transpired while he was in the Midwest.

The sweet smell of fresh baked goods and hot coffee wafted toward him when Ben opened the door to the bakery. Even though it was Monday and past the summer tourist season, they still had to stand at the end of a long line of retirees and families with children pointing at all the different candy displays. He didn't begrudge travelers from coming here in the fall. September had always been his favorite month in Lancaster County. The leaves were already turning, the air although warm held a gentle breeze, and shops were full of autumn delights.

Once they had paid for their double-scoop cones, they found a seat outside in the shade. Sam's tongue was rescuing every trickling drop from his salted caramel cone, some landing on his chin. Between laps, he peered at his brother. "So, tell me about Leah. What's she like?"

Should he sugarcoat her condition or tell him the truth? There'd been too much deceit already between Sam and Leah. He deserved to know the truth. "She's pretty and very tiny. You could pick her up and put her in your pocket. Brynn, her sister, told me she used to be a cheerleader in high school, but now she has to use a cane because she has rheumatoid arthritis, so her life is…limited because she can't do the things she used to be able to do." He studied his brother's reaction to see if his message was getting through. Life would not be easy for either one of them.

His face sobered, and he placed the remains of his cone in the trash, then took a rag out of his pocket to wipe his hands and face. "That's why I want to take care of her. She needs me. What is the disease like?"

"Well, you know our Daed has arthritis in his knees, which keep him for putting weight on them. That's why he has good days and bad days. He says it's the approach of the storm. Could be. I don't know." Ben took a quick tongue swipe of his ice cream before it toppled onto the table. The late morning sun was doing a number on their treats. "But Daed doesn't have RA. If he did, he'd need to see a doctor regularly and take prescription drugs, which of course, he would refuse to do. Rheumatoid arthritis gets worse with time, but if it's caught early enough, the damage can be prevented. In Leah's case, she's probably at stage 3." He stood to throw away what was left of his cone.

"What does that mean?"

He returned to the table and looked Sam square in the face. "It means there's no more cartilage between the bones, so they rub together, which causes pain, swelling, and loss of movement. The bones may even become disfigured. It usually hits the toes and fingers, which makes it hard to do simple tasks." His head tilted slightly. "If you brought her here, you couldn't be part of the Amish community unless she agreed to be baptized, and you know what that means."

He nodded. "I'd be shunned. It would kill Daed and Mamm, but what can I do? I love her and I want to take care of her. I can still work on the farm if he'll let me. If not, I can find a job in town. I could even drive one of those tourist buggies."

"Well, pray about it. The Lord will guide you to make the right decision. He always does." Ben swung his legs over the wooden seat of the picnic table. "We should get a move on. I have to take the dog home and catch up on office work." As they drove back to the farm, Samuel filled him in on what had transpired in the week he'd been gone. A dozen phone calls to return, some appointments to make, and some reports to write, and he'd be back on his schedule.

For the rest of the day he lost himself in the work waiting for him—Rhonda Keiser had called several times every day whenever she had a panic attack. As he listened to her hysterical voice in one message after another, his head thrummed. Adrian Frazier, the bipolar client who hadn't shown up for his appointment before he left, hadn't returned his phone calls. Hopefully he wasn't suffering another bout of mixed episodes—manic and depressed at the same time. The last time it happened, he had painted the whole inside of his house yellow without eating or sleeping, then slept for two days. It was time to take a trip to Adrian's place.

Once he'd read all the intake reports, returned phone calls, made appointments, and was on his way to Adrian's, an idea germinated in his mind— an idea that might resolve Samuel and Leah's conundrum. Was he meddling, or was he doing what a big brother should for a younger sibling just as Brynn had done for Leah? *Brynn*. He'd managed to keep all thoughts of her at bay while he caught up on his work, but he knew the minute he was home, she'd be front and center in his mind.

He reached a mid-century neighborhood close to the downtown area of Lancaster. Each brick house looked exactly like the next, and he had to check the address on Adrian's file to find the right house. There it was—he should have known. From the garden festooned with weeds sprouted out pansies, celosia, marigolds, goldenrod in a palette of golds, vibrant reds, and orange—Adrian's handiwork during a manic period. The weeds surrounding them testified to Adrian's present condition.

Before knocking on the door, he prayed that Adrian wouldn't shut him out and that he'd be able to help him this time. The first few knocks and a phone call yielded no results. He wiggled the door knob. It opened. Should he go in? Steeling himself for what awaited him, he called out his name. No response. Stepping in, he called his name again, then stopped to listen.

The sound of television voices. He called out and waited. The stale air begged for an open window. This place probably didn't have air conditioning. A few steps took him to the galley kitchen overflowing with dirty dishes and fast-food containers. Fruit flies circled the garbage and lit on some overripe bananas. Normally Adrian kept a tidy house. This didn't bode well.

Ben passed through the living room where a pillow and blanket sat in a pile on the couch just like last time Adrian had gone into a funk. He'd slept the days and nights away once his body gave out after the painting marathon. This time there was no evidence of any type of marathon. With an intake of a breath, Ben leaned his ear close to the bedroom door for any sound of movement. The only sound came from the canned laughter of a sitcom. He knocked on the door. No response. What was waiting for him on the other side? Was he too late? His heart was beating at warp speed. *Lord, I need your help.*

Inching it open, the only thing he could see was the TV set that sat on the dresser. Turning on the light, his eyes landed on a mountain of bedsheets and blankets covering what appeared to be his client, his dark hair peeking out from a pillow. Ben waited momentarily for any sign of life—the rise and fall of the body—*any movement, Lord.* And then the sweet sound of a snore reached his ears. Alive. *Thank you.* Nothing else mattered.

The room was a colossal mess with clothes, magazines, and who-knows-what on the floor. Potato chips spewed out of its bag and littered the nightstand. A cup of coffee with a layer of congealed cream sat next to the lamp. Absent was a bottle of pills, which was a good thing.

He gently shook Adrian's shoulder which resulted in a growl. "Go away. I'm trying to sleep."

"C'mon, Adrian. It's Dr. Fisher. Time to get up." The line, 'you can sleep when you die,' seemed slightly inappropriate, so he held it back. His patients didn't aways get or appreciate his morbid humor.

After another round of shaking him, Adrian finally flipped over, shielding his eyes from the light. "What are you doing here?"

"I was worried about you. You didn't show up for your appointment last week, and I haven't heard from you."

"I'm fine. Just tired. I'll call you next week. Don't worry." He covered his head with his pillow and flipped back over.

"What about your job at the school?"

"I called in sick a few days ago. The other janitors can fill in for me." his muffled voice growled. "Turn out the light on your way out."

He wasn't ready to yield the battle. "When was the last time you ate?"

"Turn out the light," Adrian rasped.

"Okay, but if you don't call me by tomorrow, I'll be back. And you need to clean this place up. It stinks." He turned out the light and stepped out of the room. Should he? Rex could probably hold it for another hour, and the kind of mess in this place would make anyone stay in bed. He pushed up his sleeves and filled the sink with sudsy water.

Ninety minutes later, the whole place smelled of Pine Sol, every garbage bag was full and sitting on the side outside the back door, and the counters gleamed. A glimpse in the fridge showed the need for groceries. When he returned in a few days, he'd come with a few bags of essentials. It was hard for loners like Adrian, who had no family to check up on them. He'd have to play that role until he was back on his feet.

A yawn escaped as he took the dog out for a quick walk around the block. What he needed was a good night sleep, but he already knew sleep would be a long time coming. The idea that had begun to germinate as he was doing dishes and sweeping the floor at Adrian's house was now growing to the point that he needed to think it through, maybe even write it down.

Once back at the house, he grabbed a can of soda from the fridge and took it to the deck outside his kitchen. The September sun was already slipping behind the tree beyond his fence. What would Brynn think of his idea? Was it too late to call her? Was this so-called plan running through his head another name for meddling in his brother's business? He always warned his clients about making plans without thinking them through. Here he was doing the same thing, but wasn't time of the essence?

Chapter Ten

"The heart is deceitful above all things, and
desperately wicked. Who can know it?"
~ Jeremiah 17:9

Work had been the therapy Brynn needed to erase thoughts of the man who'd taken a significant place in her life, then like a wisp of a cloud, had vanished. She should have known better. It could never work between the two of them. They lived 686.2 miles apart, at least that's what Google had told her. It could have been 5000 miles because their work would always keep them apart. Add to that the fact he hadn't called in three days. In fact, she hadn't heard from him since he'd left.

At least she'd obtained two estimates on the damage to the rooms, and her insurance company would cover everything but the deductible. Only a handful of people registered to stay at the hotel, which was normal for weekdays in late September. With time on her hands and no desire to think too much, she'd decided to retile her kitchen and bathroom floors, which was a lot more complicated than she'd anticipated. Another case of not counting the cost before taking on a project. She blew a strand of hair out of her eyes as she knelt in the kitchen, her gloves covered with wet grout. What had she gotten herself into?

A strident voice blasted from the TV—something about used cars for sale under a big tent. And because her hands were covered, she couldn't even turn it off. Another foolish thing, like thinking she could fix her sister's problems. Had she just waited, her sister would have fixed them herself. Had she waited, she wouldn't have paid thousands to the scam hunters or paid twelve-hundred dollars deductible for the rooms they destroyed, or had to replace her stolen safe. Life would have gone on as it always had—predictable but satisfactory. Yes, she preferred a predictable life.

But then she wouldn't have met Ben. Her eyes stole to her phone sitting on the kitchen counter. He probably had a lot of work to catch up on. But if he felt the same way she did, nothing could have kept him from calling her the minute he'd arrived home. And that thought sliced through her like the grouting knife she held.

Brynn struggled to her feet, trying to avoid the puddles of grout on the floor. A glimpse around the mess she'd created made it clear she should have hired a professional to do the job. YouTube videos made it look so easy, but they lied. Another case of scamming.

Well, enough of feeling sorry for herself. She'd take a shower then catch up on some of the sleep she'd missed. While she was stuffing wet newspapers from the floor into a trash bag, the phone rang. Not a good time since her hands were caked. If it was her sister, she'd call her back later.

No, it might be him. She pressed a baby finger on the button. "Hello?"

"Did I catch you at a bad time?" Ben. Her eyes closed. *Thank You, Lord.*

"No, it's just my hands are covered with grout. Wait a second while I wash them off."

When she returned from the sink, she offered a proper hello. "How are things?" Lame.

"Pretty good. What are you doing with grout? Are you trying to do the repairs yourself?"

His low, mellow voice sent shivers to her heart. "What? No, I just decided to redo my kitchen and bathroom floor. Didn't realize how big of a job it was." *Another bad decision.* Okay, she would not make the assumption that he was calling for any romantic reason, so she'd keep it casual. "So how's Lancaster County?"

"It's beautiful. The leaves are changing. Kind of reminds me of a certain part of Michigan." A pause ensued. Was he waiting for her to respond? As she was about to agree with him, he continued, "I miss you." His voice was so quiet.

The words spewed out. "I miss you too. I wondered if...if—"

"If I'd forgotten you? Of course not. I've wanted to call, but this idea has been whizzing around in my head, and I didn't know if it's a good idea or if it was meddling. That's why I haven't called. I wanted to wait until I had a firm confirmation that I was doing the right thing."

"What thing?" She sidestepped a puddle and lowered into a chair at the dinette table. Whatever he said was going to be just fine with her. Ah, she was so smitten.

"Well, it seems my brother is smitten—" Her gasp interrupted him mid-sentence.

"Sorry, I was just thinking that same word—smitten—in my head." She winced. Too much information. "You mean he's smitten with my sister?"

"Sure is. Like a woebegone puppy. Samuel's the epitome of pining." His sigh was loud enough to span several states. "So I want your opinion about what I've been batting around in my head. What would you say to bringing your sister to Amish country for a face-to-face with my brother? I think they'd make a good couple. They're both lonely and not sure of themselves. Maybe meeting in person would help them decide one way or another. Or am I meddling?"

So this wasn't about her; it was about matchmaking their siblings. She could feel her spirits deflate. Yet he had said he missed her. But that could be what any friend would say to another. He was waiting for a response. "I don't know. My track record hasn't been so good with interfering in Leah's life. How about I propose the idea to her. She's afraid of flying so we'd have to drive there…" Her voice trailed off. Maybe he didn't care about how they'd get there. This was going to be so hard, trying to read his intentions.

"I would love the chance to show you my life out here. But would you be able to take more time away from the motel?"

Could she? Yes, but would she, when all he wanted to do was help his brother? Would Ben have even called if he hadn't come up with his plan? "It's pretty slow now, so I could manage it. Milli and her husband, Brett, are here to oversee the work on the two rooms. Let me talk to Leah, and see if she feels the same way about Samuel. I wouldn't want your brother to be hurt if she didn't return his feelings. He doesn't know about your plan, does he?"

"No, and I won't tell him until you're on your way. He's very shy, so I almost think it would be best to surprise him. What do you think?"

Flashes of an old TV show played in her head of surprise visits and how they didn't usually end well. "A couple of years ago, there was a show called *Catfish*, where they'd bring together two people who had been in an online relationship. Most of the time, one had lied about their identity, and usually it didn't end well. But our sibs have come clean about who they really are. I'll talk to Leah, and see what she says. What do you hope will happen?"

"That they'll fall deeply in love, get married, and live happily ever after. But they both come from different worlds, and I'm not sure if they would be committed enough to step into a new one."

Was he talking about their future as well? Maybe it would be good to see how things really stood in his world, and if she was honest, she wanted as much time as she could with the man who had captured her heart. "Okay, I'll talk to her." Was this it? "I guess we'll be talking soon."

An awkward pause followed. "Okay, well, it's good to hear your voice. Bye." Click.

For the longest time, she stared at her phone, trying to make sense of it. What she wouldn't do to be able to read people's minds. Maybe if she had, she'd have known that Jess Cooper and his Houghton Lake posse were scammers. And more importantly, she'd know whether Ben Fisher loved her. *Loved her*? Because she loved him.

A few minutes later, she called her sister. Sometimes, Leah didn't answer if she was taking a nap, which happened more and more often lately. Research online had revealed that many people with stage 4 RA lived normal lives. A friend of hers even coached a community soccer team. Was her sister just giving up because she had nothing to live for?

Leah answered on the fifth ring just before it went to voicemail. "Hello?" her voice was breathy.

"Hi, Leah, what are you doing?" Tiptoeing out of the kitchen, she lowered onto a recliner and pulled her legs underneath her. Maybe if she just listened, she'd find the answers she was looking for.

"Good. A local church just dropped off a boatload of food—a whole chicken, a bag of potatoes, some canned goods, and a dozen blueberry muffins. They just drove up and down the street and left a bag at my door. I can live off this for a month."

"That's great." She flinched at the thought her sister was living on charity, but Brynn had invited her to move in with her, and she declined. Said she didn't know anyone in Saugatuck. How would she react to the idea of moving across the country if it worked out between her and Samuel? Get to the point. "How's your Amish guy?"

"He's great. We talked about two hours last night. He finally told me his name. Samuel Fisher. Ben's brother. He told me all about his childhood. How he only went to eighth grade, but Sam said he had to help his dad on the farm. It's funny. When I was in ninth grade, I used to skip all the time. Wonder if I would have appreciated it more if I couldn't go. Hmm."

Brynn scratched at a bit of grout on her hand. "I think we take a lot for granted. So it sounds like you enjoy talking to Samuel."

"Yeah, he's so nice to me. He always says the right thing. Not like Gary did—a lot of time he said the same thing every morning. 'Good morning, precious lamb,' and 'how's my angel doing?' I liked it at the time, but now I wonder if he even knew my name."

How to get the truth out of her sister about how she felt about him? Until she figured it out, Brynn continued to ask questions. "And how's Samuel different?"

"I don't know. Maybe it's the way we talk about more personal things—deeper things, like how we handled bullying in school and what we believe about God. Gary only wanted to know what I had for breakfast. You know what? The way Samuel describes Lancaster County, the farm he grew up on, the church he went to—it sounds so idyllic. Sometimes I wish—"

"Wish what?" Brynn said, as she worried some of the grout off her knuckle with her teeth.

"It's a simpler life. No TV. No computers or movies or cars. People work with their hands and share meals with friends and family. Maybe life would make better sense without all the distractions."

"Do you think you could live without modern conveniences?"

Leah's sigh preceded her words. "That's a good question. My TV is on all the time just for the noise because without it the silence is so loud." She chuckled. "That was deep."

"Yes, you sound like a poet." It was time to go in for the kill. "What about you and I going on a road trip? We could take our time driving to Pennsylvania and see if Bird-in-Hand is as idyllic as you think it is." Brynn waited for the huff, and there it was.

"Oh, I don't know. What if my RA acts up? And how would I get around?"

"The same way you get around here. We'd bring your wheelchair and your walker. And as I said, we wouldn't be in any hurry. I don't get a lot of guests at the motel this time of year, except on the weekends, and Milli and her husband can handle it. The leaves are changing. Ben says there are some awesome buffets in his town, and quilt shops, and county fairs. What do you say? Neither you nor I have had a vacation in years. C'mon. Just the two of us. Thelma and Louise."

"Didn't they die on the trip?"

Brynn had to laugh. "We're not going to be chased by a convoy of police cars, and I doubt if there are any cliffs in Ohio." She could tell Leah's protests were weakening. "This would be a chance to find out if Samuel is as nice as you think he is, and I know he really likes you."

Another huff. "Well, I'd have to convince the pharmacist to give me my prescriptions early, and I'd have to change some doctor's appointments..." Her voice trailed off.

"What is it?"

"What if he sees me and doesn't like me?" Her voice was quieter now.

"Don't even think that. You've already won that battle. You two know each other—really know each other better than most people do."

Chapter Eleven
"And after all, what is a lie? 'Tis but the truth in
masquerade."
~ Lord Byron

The September hues of golds and reds breezed past as Brynn traveled to meet her sister's future. Even if they weren't on a trip with an important destination, every mile of the journey was therapy for both of them. Since Mom had died two years ago, necessity made them sequester their grief and get on with the urgent. Neither one of them had really talked in all that time.

Her sister was as excited as a six-year-old on Christmas morning. "Oh, look at that!" she repeated, pointing this way and that. Yes, this trip was long overdue. They could have made the trip in one long day of driving, but it would be better to arrive in Bird-in-Hand when they weren't travel weary. After a good sleep and a shower, they'd be at their best when they saw Ben and Samuel.

They talked about all sorts of things. Memories from high school, long-lost friends, how they missed their mother. At first Brynn made sure she pulled in to every rest stop so her sister could stretch her legs. If Leah sat too long in the same position, her body would stiffen up.

Then lunchtime came, and everything changed.

As she circled to the back of the car to pull out the wheelchair, Leah stopped her. "No, I think I can make it on my own."

What? "But what if you fall?"

"I'll be fine. If you want, I can take my walker, but I'm pretty sure I can manage on my own."

Who was this person? They walked at a slow pace, side by side, Brynn ready to catch her if she fell. By reflex she linked arms with Leah, just in case, but her sister pulled her arm loose. "No, I can do it."

Once they were at the table perusing the lunch menu, she couldn't help but ask her sister what was going on.

Leah's eyes peeked over the menu. "I'm trying to do things on my own so Samuel won't see my disability; he'll see me." Her eyes crinkled. "And I did it."

"Yes, you did, Leah. Yes, you did." She only hoped Leah wasn't so intent on impressing him she pushed herself too far.

Back in the car, they decided to stop for the night in Youngstown, Ohio, which was just a few hours from Bird-in-Hand. How she loved the name of the Amish town, and she couldn't wait to see its psychologist up close and personal. This trip was not only about Leah and Samuel; it was also about Ben and her future. She hoped things would be crystal clear once she saw him. If it was over between them, then she'd know instead of pining. But until then, she'd think of different things. "Did you ever send Sam a picture of yourself?"

"Yeah, one from cheerleading camp. I don't have any recent ones I like."

Brynn cut a sideways glance at her. "That's over ten years old."

She gazed out the window. "Yeah, I know. But I finally got to see what Sam looks like."

"How so?"

Wincing, Leah shifted in her seat to face her. "Well, once I knew the picture he'd sent me wasn't him, I asked him to send me a real picture. But he doesn't have any. Apparently, the Amish think pictures are graven images."

"So how did you get one?"

She pointed at the side of her head with her index finger. "Always thinking. I told him to take a picture of himself with the cell phone he was using. He didn't know how, so I talked him through pushing the little button on the bottom to turn the screen around, then he took it and sent it to me."

Her eyes darted quickly at her sister and back to the road ahead. "So show me already."

"He's good-looking. Really big, and he has gorgeous eyes and a square jaw." She scrolled through her pictures and turned the phone to face Brynn. "See for yourself."

A quick glance showed a contemplative young man, his eyes were blue but looked like they carried the weight of the world. A straw hat shaded most of his face, but it was smooth, including the space above his lips. "What do you think of him?"

"He kind of reminds me of Charles in *Little House on the Prairie*. Rugged, wise, kind. He's wearing suspenders and a cowboy hat just like Charles did in the show. The way Samuel describes his life there, it sounds like paradise. I can see myself living there. Sitting on the porch shelling beans, skimming the fat off of fresh milk."

"Ew. You've never shelled a bean in your life, and you don't even like milk. Remember how you always found a way to spill your milk growing up?" Was Leah's fascination with the Amish lifestyle due to her dissatisfaction with her own life, or was God preparing for a big change?

Chapter Twelve

"A little lie is like a little pregnancy—it doesn't
take long before everyone knows."
~ C. S. Lewis

"I'm here," his brother's pronouncement
was accompanied by a double knock on Ben's
slightly ajar office door. Sam stood holding his hat
in the threshold, shifting from foot to foot.

Ben could feel a smirk form. "I'm pretty sure I
knew that when I heard you open the outside door.
C'mon in."

What his brother wasn't asking but obviously
wanted to know was why Ben had summoned him
to his office at noon instead of later in the afternoon
as was his usual schedule.

"Daed's not feeling well, so I don't have very
long. What do you n-need me to do?"

Good question. Should he just tell him that the
love of his life would be here in mere minutes, or
should he make something up? A bit of both would
suffice. "I have a little surprise for you but not quite
yet. Meanwhile, would you return these phone calls
for me and see if you can set up some
appointments?"

With a sigh, Sam peered out the window. "I

really need to go back. I have to bring the soybeans in because a frost is expected in a few days. And with Daed having t-trouble with his knees, it'll take me twice as long."

Even though Ben had a lot of reports to file and a few clients to call, his brother and father needed more assistance than he did. Up until now Daed hadn't let him help. But maybe he should insist. His timing to bring Brynn and her sister to town was way off. "How about *I* help with the harvest? Daed doesn't need to know. Between the two of us, we could finish the job in a few afternoons."

Samuel's head cocked to the side. "If he caught you, who knows what he'd do to both of us?"

Ben stood when he heard a car brake in the parking lot and joined his brother. "Let me worry about that." Brushing some hay off of Sam's shoulders, he slid past him and went to the front door. Female voices came from just outside. He opened it. The moment his eyes landed on Brynn, his heart started palpitating. He took a measured breath. She was, indeed, the one, but how could he convince her of it? Brynn was so independent. Would she give it all up for a life with him? Or would he desert his family for a life with her?

Her beatific smile. The reddish sheen of her hair. The way she rested her hand on her sister's shoulder to steady her as they approached the door. He longed to take her in his arms, and let their siblings handle their own relationship, but he'd started this, so it was up to him to finish it. "Welcome to Bird-in-Hand. C'mon in, you two. I have someone I want you to meet."

As Brynn passed him, he pulled her close into a side embrace and kissed her temple, the scent of shampoo and soap delighting his senses. "It's so good to see you. I missed you."

"Good to see you too." She stood on the other side of the door, letting her sister enter.

"Hi, Ben." Leah leaned in as he gave her an awkward hug. "So this is your office?"

"Yes, it is. Thanks for meeting me here. Did you have a good trip?"

"Oh, it was wonderful," she enthused. "The scenery—the leaves were so, so…" Her hand went to her mouth.

Just as Ben had envisioned it, their eyes locked on each other for the first time. Samuel stood there, staring, his eyes unreadable while Leah froze, not moving from the door.

Finally, Samuel took a few slow steps toward her. "Leah. I…I didn't know."

She visibly swallowed. "It was their idea. Are you…disappointed? We can go."

He took a few more steps. The difference in their height was at least a foot. "No, I've wanted to… to see you for a long time."

It was then that Ben realized he'd been holding his breath. He cut a sideways glance at Brynn and motioned outside. She nodded and headed out before him. Turning to his brother, he said, "We're going to take a little walk to give you two time alone. When we return, how about I treat you to lunch at the buffet across the street?"

When his brother didn't respond, Ben closed the door behind him. He hoped his brother would talk to him again. This was definitely the last time he'd play matchmaker. Taking Brynn's hand, he led her down the sidewalk. "I thought we could go to the park or check out a few shops. What do you think? How was your trip?" He had so many questions.

"As Leah said, it was wonderful. It's been a long time since the two of us have done anything together outside of an occasional dinner at a restaurant. We needed this. *I* needed this." She stopped at the display window of a craft store. "Oh, look at those wooden toys. This whole town is lovely—a throwback to former, more innocent times." She sniffed deeply. "The air is even fresher here."

"Sometimes it smells like manure." He was just about to pull her into a hug when she grabbed his hand and led him to J & R's Country Store.

"Oh, wouldn't those flower arrangements look great on the tables of the breakfast room? I'm going to buy them all."

Ben allowed her to lead him from store to store, and soon his arms were laden with so many bags he begged her to let him take them back to her car. As they walked toward his office, he spoke through the bags covering his chest. "I've reserved a suite for you two at the Bird-in-Hand Lodge. If you'd like we can check you in now and take your bags to your room, so you don't have to worry about it later. The hotel's next to the place where we're having lunch."

Her head tilted. "What would people think?"

Her question caught him off guard. "Oh, I

didn't think about that. In a town this small, it would be all over the county by the time we moved the suitcases into the room. We're probably already being watched." He laughed. "I don't mind, do you?" Once they put the shopping bags in the back seat of her car, Ben pulled her toward a bench. "Did I make a mistake by inviting you here?" That didn't come out right; he knew it the minute the words spewed out.

Furrows formed on her forehead. "What do you mean? Are you having misgivings?"

He framed her face with his hands. "By no means. I have missed you so much. What I meant was do you think I made a mistake by orchestrating the meeting between your sister and my brother?"

Her shoulders lifted, but she closed her eyes and pressed her cheek against the palm of his hand. "She was eager to see this town. I think she's in love with the idea of living a simpler life. And she likes everything about Samuel. Time will tell."

"And how do *you* like it here?"

Her eyes made a slow arc of the area. "At first glance, I find it charming." Just then her stomach gurgled. "Oh, sorry about it."

He checked his watch. "Okay, they've had forty-five minutes. Let's go get them."

The moment they walked into the office, Samuel bolted to his feet, and Leah swiped strands of hair away from her face.

"It's just us. You two ready to go for lunch? Brynn's stomach is making enough music to awaken the dead. Ouch," he said as she playfully slapped his arm.

"You are such an exaggerator."

They decided on the restaurant across the street instead of the smorgasbord since Sam had to hurry back to work. The restaurant was crowded with tourists and locals, but they managed to score a booth. They pored over their menus and ultimately ended up ordering what Ben suggested—pot roast melt sandwiches and the soup of the day.

While they waited for their soup and sandwiches, the conversation revolved around their trip and some of the local places to visit. The girls' eyes sparkled as they gazed at their surroundings and eavesdropped on the German conversations around them.

As Hannah, their server, set bowls of chicken noodle soup before them and a basket of fresh buns, her eyes held a glint as she welcomed the two women to town and asked where they were from. Now it was just a matter of time before their Mamm would know, since the two women belonged to the same quilting group. The members of this community didn't need phones to spread the word.

"Hannah, meet Leah and Brynn. They are sisters from Michigan." Ben gestured at each. "Ladies, this is Hannah Stoller, who is our—what would you say, Hannah—our third cousin on our mother's side?"

Hannah's face broke into a warm smile and greeted them as she placed melted pot roast sandwiches and french fries next to each bowl of soup. "Third or fourth. It's very nice to meet you ladies. You let me know if these lads give you a moment of trouble. They're not too big to take over my knee."

Ben cut a glance at his brother, and they both rolled their eyes. "You forget we're over thirty years old now." He shook his head. "Don't pay any attention to her." Once Hannah had moved on to the next table, he took Brynn's hand and asked a blessing over the food, then they dug into their lunches.

"This is so good," crooned Leah between sips of her soup. "These noodles are homemade. Do you think I could buy some to take home with me?"

"They're available at the g-grocery store, but if we can't find them, Mamm will give you some to take back. Here, try this." Samuel said, as he finished chewing on a fry. He squirted some mayonnaise next to a puddle of ketchup by his fries, dipped one in each sauce, then offered it to Leah, who bit into it as he held it. Such an intimate move—something he'd never seen his brother do before.

Leah seemed to enjoy it because she sighed and asked for another one. Brynn's eyes gaped at her sister, a quarter of her sandwich held in midair. Obviously Ben wasn't the only one who marveled at the sweet love story unfolding before them. Of course, Sam and Leah weren't strangers; in fact, they knew each other more deeply than he and Brynn did.

Brynn's eyes locked on his. She was thinking the same thing he was. The couple needed space and time to be alone. When they had finished as much as they could of their lunches, Ben took out his wallet, fished a few bills out of it, and threw them on the table. "It's on me."

Sam must have read his mind because he blew out a breath and patted his stomach. "Thanks, bro. I'm stuffed. Leah, how about we go check out the lobby?"

Her eyes lit up. "Sure. I'd like to buy some snacks for later in our room."

He took her hand and helped her out of the booth. "We'll meet you back at your office in a half an hour." With his hand protectively placed on Leah's lower back, he guided her out of the busy restaurant.

"How about we indulge in dessert?"

"Sounds good. I could use some coffee."

He took the seat that his brother had vacated. "A lot of curious eyes around here." When Hannah whizzed past with a coffeepot, he asked her to stop by when she'd finished refilling cups down their aisle.

"What do you suggest I should order?"

"They're known for their shoofly and their peanut butter whoopie pie. I love their coconut custard pie. But they have a lot of choices. Hannah will spiel off a list." He stacked the dishes and leaned on his elbows. "Did you notice that there was no one in this room but our siblings? I've never seen anything like it."

Leaning forward, Brynn nodded. "I know. Did you notice how light on her feet my sister was? I haven't seen her like that since Marty, her husband, was alive."

Just then, Hannah darted up to the table, picked up the stack of dishes, and placed some coffee cups in front of them. "Where did your brother go? Will he be back?"

"No, they went to look around the bakery. We'd like to order some pie, please? What do you recommend?"

"Let me put these dishes down and bring a fresh pot of coffee for you. I'll be right back."

Brynn sat back and patted her stomach. "I don't know how much room's left in here. I can tell I'm going to have to start running again to lose the weight I gain while I'm here." Her eyes clouded over. He wondered if she was thinking the same thing he was. His hand slipped over hers and stayed there.

At that moment Hannah returned with fresh coffee and a bowl of creams. "Apple crumb is our pie of the day. We also are featuring a red velvet whoopie pie, but we also have lemon, coconut, shoofly, apple—I think that's it." Her eyes fell on Brynn as she poured each a cup of coffee.

"I've never had shoofly pie before, so that's what I'd like, please." Brynn smiled back.

"How about I order a piece of coconut custard and we try each other's?"

"Good choices, lovebirds. I'll be right back." She covered her lips. "I won't tell." With a wink, she breezed away.

He leaned forward again. "She won't have to. A dozen people will find a reason to stop by and visit Mamm today. Is that okay with you?"

"I'm okay with it. Is it okay with you? These are your people."

"It's okay with me because I'm not part of the

old-order any more, but my brother is the one who will have to undergo the scrutiny of the members of the congregation. He's taken a big leap today. I hope he's ready for it."

Once Hannah had brought their desserts, Brynn bit into hers, closed her eyes, and moaned. "This is scrumptious." After taking a sip of her coffee, she put her cup down. "I thought you said your brother had a speech impediment."

"Sam's always stuttered, especially when he's nervous." He blew out a breath. "He didn't today."

"I know. Maybe they're two pieces of a puzzle that just needed to find each other to be whole." She took a bite of his pie when he offered, savored it with the slow toss of her head. "Pie takes on a whole new meaning here."

He stared at her until she opened her eyes. "This is going down as one of my favorite memories. Having you here with me. Seeing your delight. How long can you stay?" Forever?

But no, she had a business to run.

"Maybe two more days. I have imposed on Milli too much lately. Could we just walk outside for a few minutes? It's so beautiful, and I want to take in as much as I can in the time I have here...with you."

After adding a twenty to the pile on the table, he stood, then followed her out of the restaurant and onto the sidewalk that lined Old Philadelphia Pike. For the first time in his life, he didn't care what the neighbors said; he took her hand as they strolled down the street. "Since it's Monday, a lot of the shops are closed, but we can window browse." It didn't matter what setting they were in as long as she was next to him. Without intending to, he squeezed her hand.

A horse-drawn buggy passed on the shoulder close to them, the air filling with equine scents. A convertible sped past making the horse's head jerk to the right. At the sight, Brynn covered her mouth and froze. "That poor horse. What was the driver thinking? Clearly he saw the buggy."

"The horses are used to it. The worst is when the cars slow down to take pictures. It's very upsetting, but it happens all the time." At the corner he pulled her onto a quieter road, the ones tourists rarely traveled. A few blocks down, they passed his old school, scooters lining the fence in the playground. "This is where I went to school up to eighth grade."

Stopping at the chain-linked fence, she whistled. "Oh, it's like something out of a storybook. An ode to a simpler time, a purer time. I wish we could see it on the inside."

"There's a place not far from here where you can take tours of an Amish community. Maybe you and your sister can do that while we're working tomorrow." He glanced at his watch. "Sam needs to get to work. Once you two are settled in your room, I'm going to go help him for a few hours. It's the least I can do after what he did for me while I was in the Midwest."

She reached up and did the unexpected—she kissed him on his cheek. His hand automatically went to cover the spot. "I love it here," she said, "and I—" Just then a buggy clopped by, and she whirled around to see it, her eyes wild with delight.

"And you what?"

"Oh, nothing. I just feel like I'm in this dream, and I don't want to wake up."

Hang roving eyes. He was going to kiss her now, but not in front of the school. "Come here, you." He pulled her a few feet from full view of the school window. How often had he stared out of the same window during times drills and memory-verse recitation? Back then even the flitting leaves looked as if they were having more fun. He pulled her behind an American beech tree and enfolded her in his arms. "May I welcome you properly to Lancaster County, Ms. Kingston?"

"Why, yes, you may, kind gentleman." When their lips met, it was like coming home. Her lips supple, her hair resplendent—so luscious he could lose himself in it. And before he knew it, "I love you," escaped from his own lips, carried on a breath—the first time he'd ever said those words to anyone but his family.

Inches apart, their eyes opened at the same time. He could see his reflection in her irises. There. He'd said it, and he couldn't take it back. Now he had to be ready when she said she just wanted to be friends, or something practical. He waited. It was better to know now than to hope for the impossible. His chin lifted. "It's true. I love you. Can't deny it. Can't suppress it. It is what it is."

Her eyes clouded for a moment, then her face broke into a beautiful smile, as if those same clouds had parted revealing the sun. "And I love you," her voice so soft he almost didn't hear her. She stared above his head. "So what are we going to do about it?"

He trailed a finger down her forehead, nose, and touched her lips. "Well, we could write sappy love letters to each other, or we could spend hours on the phone every night, saying, 'you hang up. No, you hang up.' Or we could do something else. What are your thoughts?"

She leaned against the tree, her hands behind her back. "All those things you mentioned are fine things, but I don't think they'd last for very long."

He brushed a strand of hair away from her forehead. "You take the romance right out of it. I say we pray about it, and the Lord will give us some concrete answer to our dilemma."

"Sounds like a perfect solution." She closed her eyes and pursed her lips, which he gladly met until a honk of a car and a voice yelled, "Get a room."

Ben spun her around. "He's right. Not about the room but about meeting my brother back at the office so I can drive him home. Let's go."

Fifteen minutes and they were back at the office. He tried to open the door, but it was locked. Was his brother inside? Maybe he'd forgotten his key. Ben knocked on the door. Giggling came from the other side. Ben cut a curious glance at Brynn, who also looked suspicious. The door opened and there stood Samuel with his arm around Leah.

"Why'd you lock the door?" Ben stood back so Brynn could precede him. The look on his brother's face was something he'd never seen before and couldn't define if he tried. Leah looked like she'd swallowed a canary, although the cliché broke down when it came to humans. "What's up, you two?" he asked as they entered the reception area.

Leah peered up at Sam. "Can I tell him?" When he nodded, she linked her arms with him. "Guess what? Samuel asked me to marry him, and I said yes."

Chapter Thirteen

Honesty is often very hard. The truth is often
painful.
But the freedom it can bring is worth the trying."

~ Fred Rogers

Leah hadn't stopped talking since they'd checked into their hotel room and had taken showers. It was as if she'd come alive after a long hibernation. Now as she brushed through the tangles of her freshly shampooed hair, she recounted how the minute they'd closed the office door behind them, he'd locked it, pulled her into his arms, and professed his love for her.

"He said he'd been waiting his whole life for me, so why waste another moment? 'Marry me now, as soon as possible. I love you so much I don't want to live another day without you.' It was so romantic." She whirled around and dropped onto one of the two queen beds.

Happy for her sister, Brynn let her relive it. "Then what did you say?"

"I told him I loved him, and I said yes three times."

Brynn plopped on her own bed and toweled her

hair. "So what happens next?"

"Tomorrow morning, Sam will pick me up in a buggy, and we'll go meet his parents." She breathed in. "I'm so nervous. What if they don't like me? What if they say no?"

She set the towel down, plugged in Leah's curling iron, and picked up a brush. "It's not a matter of them not liking you; it's a matter of you being English. They don't allow their children to marry outside of their culture. You need to be ready for them not to welcome you with open arms."

She tossed her head. "I'm not going back to Michigan, Brynn. I'm staying right here, and I'm going to join their church or whatever they call it. They believe the same things we do, I think. So they'll be happy when they realize I'm going to be baptized Amish. Then Samuel won't have to leave his family. He can still help his father, and I'll get to live in this bit of paradise."

Brynn didn't want to be a downer, but Leah's rose-colored glasses kept her from seeing the negative possibilities. But Brynn had to try. "Leah, two things to consider. Life on a farm is hard work. Everything is made from scratch. You won't have a microwave or a television or even the curling iron you're using. You'll have to get up while it's still dark to make Samuel's breakfast. What about your RA? How will you be able to shell beans when your fingers are stiff and sore?"

There it was—the eye roll. Sometimes she felt more like Leah's mother than her sister.

"Way to bring me down. You always do that. I know it's going to be a whole new learning curve for me. But anything's better than sitting all day in that trailer. Trust me for once, Brynn, and be happy for me. Samuel's mother will be there to teach me how to cook. And all the women in the church will be there as well."

She shifted her legs so she faced her sister. "Okay, I'll trust you. But I just have one more thing. You're an outsider, even if you do get baptized and join their church. They speak a different language when they're together. Some form of German. And not everyone will welcome you. Are you up to that kind of rejection? Do you realize I won't even be allowed to come to your wedding?"

She nodded. "I thought about that. It bothers me you won't be nearby. But it's time I put on my big girl pants—or more appropriately—my big girl skirt. It's time for me to grow up."

Taking both of her hands, Brynn held them in hers, realizing for the first time this may be their last two nights together. Tears sprang unannounced or invited. "You're right. It's going to be hard not having you an hour away. I'm going to miss you so much. Who am I going to rescue now?"

Leah swiped at her face. "Well, you could always move here and marry Ben. I wouldn't be able to talk to you since you'd be shunned, but we could pass secret messages to each other. Or maybe you could join the church and convince Ben to do the same. And then we could have so much fun here quilting and tatting—isn't that some kind of needlework?"

"Well, back to the real world, girl. I'll be

leaving the day after tomorrow, so do you have any idea where you're going to stay if you don't go back with me?"

As was their tradition whenever they had a sleepover, Leah lifted her foot to rest on Brynn's lap and rummaged through her makeup kit, unearthing a bottle of apple-red nail polish. "It might be the last time, so do a good job."

"All right, but I'm not going to do your fingernails. That's probably *verboten*."

"I know that German word. See? I'll be able to carry on a short conversation." She giggled and waved a dismissive hand. "In response to your question, I'll know more after I meet with his parents. Wish you could go with me, but Samuel will be there. Did you notice he only stuttered a few times?"

She shook the bottle. "I did. And you were walking all over the place as well."

"Well, it caught up with me while we were at the bakery, so we cut it short and took our time going back to the office. But I have to say I feel pretty great." She clapped her hands. "Brynn, I'm getting married. Be happy for me."

She peered up and smiled. "I am very happy for you." But was she? Did her sister have a clue what she was getting into? It would be hard for an able-bodied woman to join a culture that might not be so welcoming, but how much more for her disabled sister?

Chapter Fourteen
"A lie that is a half-truth is the darkest of all lies."
Alfred Lord Tennyson

Brynn had no clue what tenterhooks were, but she was on them as she waited for her sister to call to tell her how Sam's parents had reacted to the news. The only call she'd received was from Ben, who invited her to have lunch and spend the afternoon with him on this, their last day together. Never had she thought she'd be returning home alone. Never had she thought she'd even consider putting the for sale sign in front of the motel, but right now it seemed like a weight around her neck, keeping her from being with the man she loved.

But she had to wear her big-girl skirt and run her business the best she knew how until God told her otherwise.

Since this was their last day together, she spent a bit more time on her hair, gave herself an extra spritz of cologne, and practiced smiling in front of the mirror, although that was the last thing she wanted to do. Her sister had left an hour earlier when Samuel had picked her up in his family's buggy. How romantic for her.

Her phone buzzed a message from Ben that

said he was waiting in the parking lot in a dark gray Hyundai Santa Fe. She grabbed a sweater, though from the moment she stepped outside, the warm September breeze informed her she wouldn't need it. The dark SUV was sitting under the porte cochère, its engine running. Understanding Ben's need for anonymity, she hurried to the passenger side and climbed in, hoping she'd picked the right vehicle.

"Good morning, sunshine." He grinned, his faced sporting a growing garden of stubble.

"Are you growing a beard?"

His hand brushed over his cheek. "No, I'm just making the most of my last day off for a while. How would you like to take a drive into the country? We have about two dozen covered bridges that are still standing. Sam and Leah will be meeting us at three at the office to tell us how it went with the parents, so that gives us a few hours…to hang out."

Rows of quilt shops and markets and hotels whizzed past. It was quaint but definitely targeted at tourists. They turned onto a narrow road, and everything changed. Farm houses sat close to the road on one side, hobby farms behind them, while on the other side, simpler houses with no window treatments sat back from the road. Clotheslines full of garments extended from an upstairs-window pulley to a tree. "What a great idea. They don't even have to go outside to collect their clothes; they can just wheel them in."

"Yes, my Mamm has one. You might have noticed the houses on the left are different than the ones on the right. The Old Order Amish families live on the left, and the Mennonites live on the right."

She looked at them with new eyes. "Oh, yes, I see it now. What are Mennonites?"

He put down his window and leaned his elbow out of it. "The Mennonites broke away from the Amish a century ago. Basically their beliefs are the same, but the Mennonites are more worldly. I'm a member of a Mennonite church. We can go to college, travel in cars and planes, and anyone can attend our churches."

The last thought evoked a sigh from her. "I won't be able to attend my own sister's wedding, will I?"

He glanced her way. "What? You'll be able to go to the wedding ceremony at the house; you just won't be able to go to the church service. I don't know if I'll be able to go to either, though."

That just seemed wrong to her. How could that family turn their back on their son? She'd never understand it.

"Here comes one of my favorite things— roadside stands. They're selling fresh cider and doughnuts at the house coming up. You find the best food at these little stands. Would you like to stop for some cider?"

"Oh, please, that sounds great." He pulled over onto the grass. A fortyish woman stood barefoot next to a large glass container of cider. She had such a natural beauty it was hard to tell her age with her hair covered by a white bonnet, her light blue dress enshrouded in a white apron.

"It's good to see you, Martha. How's Albert doing since his appendix operation?"

"Ach. He's ready to get back to work. Doesn't know what to do with himself, that man, sitting in the kitchen." She turned to Brynn. "May I pour you some cider? It's from our own apples. The doughnuts were fresh out of the oven this morning." Her smile was lovely. How could Brynn refuse?

As Ben and Martha chatted about local matters, Brynn's eyes took in the whole vista. The patchwork quilt of farms. The distant crow of a rooster. The clop-clop of a horse leading a buggy. She suppressed her desire to turn and stare. She sniffed of fallish scents—earthy smells. Fresh aromas. Soon they were back on the road, sipping their drinks and getting powdered sugar all over the upholstery.

A few miles took them to their first covered bridge which spanned a river. They stepped out of the SUV and approached the brown wooden, single-lane bridge. "This one is called Hunsecker's Mill Covered Bridge, built in 1848. It's the biggest of the bunch."

"How many are in the bunch?" They posed by the stone wall as he snapped a picture.

"About two dozen. Let's try to visit five this time. Save the rest for other times?" His eyebrows shifted up and down.

Yes! There would be more visits. After stopping to take selfies at four more bridges, she was smitten with Lancaster county and the man who lived there. They stopped at a roadside café, shared a sandwich, and she didn't remember anything about the place or the food except Ben. How could she possibly leave, not knowing when or if she'd ever see him again? They talked about their faith, their views on family, having children, but she had one more question. "You had said before if God wanted us together, He'd let us know. How?"

"I don't know. For me, a Bible verse pops out, and I immediately know it's the answer I've been looking for. It might be different for you."

She pushed her plate away and leaned closer. "Well, how do you know where to start reading? Do you just flip the Bible open and point?"

He swirled a french fry in ketchup. "No, I read a chapter a day every morning. I just started again at the beginning of Genesis about a month ago. I'll know it when I see it because it will pop out."

She took a sip of her water. "I like that—'I'll know it when I see it.'" In fact, maybe she'd read more than a chapter each night. Then the answer would come quicker. Or not. Why did time speed by so fast when she needed it to slow down? They arrived back at the office with minutes to spare before Samuel and Leah showed up. As they pulled into the parking lot, she shifted to face Ben. "Do you think everything went okay for them?"

He turned off the engine. "Since your sister is willing to be baptized, they'll welcome her. Mamm will love having Leah join their household. That's what I believe will happen, since Sam will be working on the farm. But it might be a different story with my sisters-in-law and some of the women in the congregation. They don't easily welcome outsiders."

As soon as they were inside the office, the sound of horse's hooves sounded close to the office. What would Leah's face reveal about how her morning had gone? Brynn hoped it wouldn't exacerbate her RA.

They walked in, Samuel's arm enveloping Leah's small frame. He would be her protector—Brynn could already tell, and Leah would need a protector. Yet at the moment her face was devoid of anything but sheer joy.

"Judging from your smile, it must have gone well," Brynn said as she hugged her sister.

"Why don't we go into my office. Then we don't have to line up in the chairs by the wall." Ben opened the door, turned on the light, and stood back as they entered. This was the first time she'd seen his office. One could tell a lot about a person by the pictures on the wall, but there were none. Still it was small and comfortable with a desk, a bookshelf, and a cluster of furniture off to the side.

Ben moved his rolling desk chair away from behind his desk and motioned for Leah and Sam to sit on the loveseat and Brynn next to him in the winged-back chair. He steepled his fingers, probably the way he did with his clients. "So it must not have gone too bad. Do tell."

Samuel's arm rested above Leah's head. Even sitting, he was much taller than she. "They were sh-shocked at first. I could tell they were curious about how I had m-met an English girl from Michigan, but they didn't ask. It w-will come up though later on."

"What are going to tell them?" Ben asked.

"The truth. Th-they were relieved when Leah told them she wanted to be baptized and join the church. Mamm's face lit up like a lantern."

Brynn broke in. "Leah, how did you feel?"

"Scared. At first they didn't even look at me. But then when I told them my plans, Mrs. Fisher came over and took my hands in hers and said, 'Welcome to the family.' She was nice."

Ben stood and shook his brother's hand. "Congratulations, I'm happy for you, Sam. So when's the big day?" He glanced at Brynn, sending her a message she couldn't decipher.

Sam took Leah's hand. "We don't want to wait, so we'll be married the first Tuesday in October at the house. That means next Sunday, we'll have the meeting at our house, and the bishop will baptize Leah at that time." His eyes grew somber. "Sorry, neither of you will be able to attend, but you're both invited to the c-ceremony in October."

Leah shifted to face her sister. "Brynn, can you come back in two weeks for the celebration? I really want you to be here with me. It wouldn't be the same without you."

Leaning toward her sister, she brushed the side of Leah's face. "I wouldn't miss it for the world. But where will you be staying in the meantime?"

Instead of answering, Leah peered at Samuel, who answered for her. "She'll be staying with Mamm and Daed, and I'll move out to the w-wedding house. It will give Leah time with Mamm to learn the customs, and it will give me a chance to fix up the old wedding house for my future bride—"

Ben interrupted. "Amish weddings are well-attended ceremonies, so most farms have a wedding house for some of the guests to stay in. Sam, I'll be more than happy to help you get the house ready." He held up a hand. "Daed doesn't need to know."

Just then there was a banging on the front door. Glancing at his brother, Ben bolted to his feet and rushed from the room, followed by Sam. What could that mean? More banging. Was it one of his clients? Not knowing what to do, Brynn stood and went to the doorway.

"What is it?" Ben said as he threw open the door.

A tall, thin woman in her twenties, in plain clothes, stood in the threshold, her eyes wild and fierce. "It's Daed. He's fallen from the hayloft stairs in the barn. Mamm's with him and sent me to get Samuel. Come, Samuel, we must hurry." Her eyes met Ben's and she turned her head away.

"Is he alive? Tell me, Sarah? Is Daed alive?"

She didn't answer but lurched forward to grab her brother's hand and pulled him out.

Chapter Fifteen

"The devil can quote scripture for his purpose."
~ William Shakespeare, *The Merchant of Venice*

"I have to go." Ben peered at Brynn, raced to the desk, and grabbed his keys. "I don't care what they say; I'm going to Daed." He glanced at her again. "Pray for...all of us." The door slammed behind him.

Mere adrenaline raced through him as he raced toward the farm. He wasn't thinking straight. How could he when Daed might be injured or worse? He dialed 911. Maybe they'd already done that from the phone housed in the shanty down the street, but just in case. The operator wanted to know much more information than he could give her. He finally just said, "Send someone quick. He's in the barn."

Buggies lined the long driveway on either side, some sitting at angles on the lawn. The whole district was here already, which meant he'd have to relive the shunning and hope they wouldn't force him to leave. But most of them had a heart, and if Daed needed him, hopefully love would overcome tradition. But even his sister hadn't shown any heart.

As he slipped past a swell of his parents' friends from church, a few turned their backs, but many nodded, which filled him with momentary gratitude. Until he saw his daed, lying on the hay-strewn floor, his eyes closed, his leg bent at an abnormal angle, and his face devoid of color. Mamm held his hand in hers, her face solemn, her jaw tight. Samuel kneeled next to her, his eyes closed as the bishop who stood next to the stairs said a prayer.

Dropping to his knees, Ben took his father's other hand, kissed the rough knuckles, then when the prayer ended, he said, "Is he—?" At the same time, he touched his fingers against his Daed's carotid artery.

"He's alive," his mother said. "You should not be—"

"I love him, and I will be here with him."

Her lips tightened, but he read grace in her eyes. She understood. "What happened?"

Sam answered. "Gus had somehow climbed up in the hayloft and was meowing up a storm. Daed went up to rescue him and must have missed a step. He hit his head, so we're trying not to move him until the paramedics come."

"Looks like he broke his leg as well."

The sound of sirens was getting louder. Murmuring behind him reached his ears. His time here was limited, so he had to say it before the bishop removed him. "Daed, I love you. I will always love you, and I will be here to help Sam, so don't you worry about anything but getting well."

English voices came from outside the barn. The

ambulance must have driven right up to the door. Just then, he felt a weak squeeze of his daed's hand. When he glanced down, his father's eyes were trained on him. A slight smile turned up the corners of his lips. "I love you too, son. Now go up and get the cat." His eyes closed once more.

Those in the immediate area laughed, and his mother smiled for the first time.

"Right away, sir." As he stood, the paramedics took his place, so he backed up, then started up the stairs. About halfway up, one of the steps was leaning at a 45 degree angle, which meant his father must have fallen about eight or nine feet. Once he reached the top, Gus backed up and hissed. All the commotion below must have scared the old tabby. As there was no room to come down, he watched the paramedics take his father's vitals, gently place something around his daed's neck, then they moved him onto a gurney.

As the crowd made room for the paramedics to pass through, the bishop looked up at him. A frown covered his face, and he shook his head, but he refrained from saying anything. Good. His mother didn't need anyone else but her husband to think about. But there would be a future meeting with the bishop, he felt sure.

"Where are you taking him?" his mother asked.

"Lancaster General," came a voice outside Ben's view. "You can ride along in the ambulance. If not, follow the signs to Emergency."

Ben was about to tell his mother he would drive her there, but his brother looked up and winked at him.

"It's only seven miles. I'll take care of Mamm."

His brother was growing up. The thought eased his mind, but at the same time, hurt a bit to think he wasn't needed anymore. Well, the cat needed him, but it would take some time to gain his trust. Gus was pasted against the far wall now. Ben crept slowly toward him on his knees, wincing as a nail ripped through his jeans. The cat responded with a low growl, but he was finally able to grab him. He stroked the fur around his neck, eliciting a purr despite the cat's initial fear. "There, there. You aren't going to shun me like the rest of them, are you?"

Well, it was apparent his father was going to be off his feet for a while, if not forever. He thanked God his daed hadn't died in the fall, and he prayed that there weren't more serious injuries to his neck or back. A fractured leg could heal; a spinal issue was a whole different thing.

Once the crowd dispersed, he climbed down. Since Sam would be busy at the hospital, it was up to him to inform Brynn and Leah about the accident and drive them back to the hotel. It seemed circumstances had just changed the course of his life. Until the crops were harvested, his brother would need daily help. Usually members of the community would show up to help bring in the crops, but now was the busiest time of the year, so at least for the next few weeks, he'd be there for his brother and would catch up on his own work at night.

Brynn would understand. It was good in a way.

They'd have time apart to think things through. Someone was going to have to yield to the other. Before the accident, he'd almost decided he'd move to Saugatuck since he could set up an office anywhere, but not so for Brynn. His Amish clients who needed in-person counseling could go on the waiting list for Whispering Hope, and those who had access to phones could continue with him. But now, at least for the next few months, he'd stay where he was.

As he turned onto the main road, he had to chuckle. How ironic that two brothers would fall in love with two sisters. God had a sense of humor—eternity would be a riot! But for the time being, he and Brynn would take their time getting to know each other via telephone, texts, maybe even a few visits. Sam and Leah's marriage might be on hold until his father was back on his feet, but that was Sam's job to break the news.

As he parked the car and walked to the office door, an unbidden shudder of a sigh poured out. He wasn't ready to say goodbye to Brynn. Pasting on a poor excuse for a smile, he entered. The girls popped up from the loveseat when he came in.

Brynn hurried toward him. "How is your father?" they said in tandem.

"He'll be fine. They took him to the hospital. Sam drove my mother there. He'll be there for a while, so I'll drive you back to the hotel, but would you like to stop on the way for some dinner?"

"Sounds good," Brynn clasped his hand. "But tell us what happened. Did you see your father? Did they let you in? Is he badly hurt?"

Her hand sent a shock through his veins or nerves—he didn't understand the anatomy of it all. Just that her touch had power. *Focus.* "He fell off the stairs leading to the hayloft. Apparently, the cat had climbed up there. Gus is about twenty years old and probably couldn't climb down on his own. My daed is a softy when it comes to Gus. Daed was on his back when I arrived. There were already a lot of people from their church, including the bishop, but they let me in. I thought he was dead at first—he was so pale, but he wasn't. I got to tell him I loved him." He blinked at the memory. "And then he opened his eyes and said, 'I love you too. Now go get the cat.'" He bit his lower lip to keep it from quivering. "He's never ever said that he loved me before. Then the ambulance arrived, and they took him away. His leg is probably broken, and they were careful about lifting him because of his neck. I'll know more tomorrow after they do tests." He nodded to add emphasis to his words.

"That's good news, isn't it? He's alive, and you had a reunion of sorts with him." Her face grew solemn. "You're worried, aren't you?"

"He'll be off his feet for a while—maybe longer if there are spinal issues. So I'm going to have to help Sam with the crops for the next few weeks."

She nodded and peered at Leah. "What about your clients?"

He shrugged. "I'll do appointments in the evening and weekends." What he didn't say was that it left little time for their relationship. He'd have to find a way.

Her lips pressed together, then she nodded. "Well, let's go, so you can go to the hospital or work. And you don't have to take us to dinner. I have a car. Besides I have to pack, and I want to leave early tomorrow so I can do the whole trip in a day."

He took her arm and linked it with his. "No, I want to take you out. Things happen. Life is messy sometimes."

They climbed into his SUV, and he headed to the Bird-in-Hand for their smorgasbord. They needed to go to one of those while they were here, but then Leah spoke up.

"Ben, would you take me back to the hotel? I'm not very hungry. Maybe Sam will call me from the phone shanty, and I—well, now things may have changed for me and him. Maybe he'll want me to go back to Michigan."

He glanced at her in the rear-view mirror. "I doubt that. If anything, you'll be a comfort to my mother. Are you sure you want to go back to the room? We can bring you something from the restaurant."

"No, I have all those baked goods calling my name. I'll be fine. But one question. Do you think Samuel can pick me up in his buggy tomorrow before I have to check out? Since Brynn's leaving so early, she won't be able to take me."

He winked at her through the mirror. "Either he or I will pick you up at eleven. How's that?"

She smiled and winked back. "That will work, bro-in-law."

After he dropped her off, he peered at Brynn.

"What's your pleasure? We don't have a lot of romantic restaurants in Lancaster, but what we do have are smorgasbords. Are you up for that?"

She brightened. "Sounds good. Comfort food. We could sit on the same side of the booth if you want romance, but everyone who works there knows you, right? Are you sure you're up for that kind of scrutiny?"

"Yes." He held his head up high. "I'm ready to go public—to declare my love for you in front of all my mother's friends, and all the rest who are relatives."

~

Once the hostess led them to their booth, they did sit on the same side, but after craning their necks to see each other, he moved to the other side.

"Are you up for a little adventure?"

She waggled her eyebrows. "What do you have in mind?"

"How would you like to try some Amish dishes?"

She leaned her chin on her fist, enjoying the view. "Such as?"

"Well, there's macaroni and cheese with stewed tomatoes—"

"Like mixed together?" She shuddered. "Why destroy a good thing?"

He placed his hand on hers. "Try it...and pickled eggs, and ham balls, and—"

"Tit for tat," she said, her chin up. "You'll have to try some Michigan foods—like pasties and...Detroit pizza. I can't think of anymore, but my mom used to make me peanut butter and mayonnaise sandwiches."

"Deal. Now let's go fill our plates."

Brynn had been to many a buffet—Chinese, Golden Corral, hotel breakfasts, but nothing like this. Still her appetite was gone—probably because their time was almost over. She selected one of each of the items he'd mentioned, plus buttered noodles and a piece of fried chicken.

When they returned to the table, he took her hand, rubbed his thumb over her knuckles, and prayed for the food. She would miss this.

His eyes twinkled when she took a bite of the purple hard-boiled egg. As she chewed, she frowned. "What does this taste like? …I know—salt and vinegar potato chips. Really?"

"Different texture, though," he said as he sipped chicken-noodle soup.

They filled the moments between chewing and swallowing with local color and safe topics. Her appetite rebounded when they browsed the dessert selections, and they decided to share bites of several pies and crisps. At the end, her stomach was full, but those Sunday night doldrums were descending, knowing their time was short.

"How would you like to walk off some of the calories?" When she nodded, he took her hand, and they strolled past mom-and-pop businesses while cars sped by, leaving horse-drawn buggies in the dust.

After a few blocks, he pulled her toward a bench, a bit away from the busy street and they sat, their arms intertwined. A sigh came out without her permission. Their eyes locked, and he nodded.

"I wanted to tell you that before my daed had the accident, I was thinking about moving close to you. My business can be moved, but yours can't, of course. But then this happened, and now I have to stay here."

Brynn leaned her head on his shoulder. "I'm not looking forward to going home. It's wonderful here, and I love it." She dabbed at a bit of whipped cream on his lip. "And I love you. I've never been good at saying goodbye, so I won't. We'll pretend like I'm just saying good night, okay?"

He kissed her hair. "The time will go by fast. Do you think you'll be able to come for the wedding celebration if it's still on?"

"Oh, yes. She's all the family I have now."

He lifted her chin, and he kissed her, and the puzzle pieces fit together perfectly. She matched him sweet for sweet, passionate for passionate, but they pulled apart when voices nearby reached their ears. He raked his fingers through his hair. "Well, they must have caught us because I heard the patter of footsteps rush away. We should go before a crowd gathers." Taking her hand, they returned to the car.

The sun had vanished behind some clouds, and the sky took on a sullen tone. He braked in front of the hotel's porte-cochère and turned toward her. "The time will go quickly. We'll pretend like one of us has gone on assignment somewhere, okay?" He brushed a strand of hair away from her face.

"I'm going to read the Bible until I have an answer," she whispered.

He pulled her into a hug, kissed her temple, and

then she managed an "I love you," before jumping out.

"To the moon and back," he said.

Chapter Sixteen

"It's discouraging to think of how many people are
shocked by honesty
and how few by deceit."
~ Noel Coward

The highway at four-thirty in the morning
was dark and empty, except for the occasional semi,
which suited Brynn just fine. Sneaking out before
anyone was awake had been her way of avoiding
tearful goodbyes for as far back as she could
remember. It all started when she'd come home
during a long weekend or for a holiday break during
college. Seeing her mother standing in the doorway
as she pulled out of the driveway, her sad face as
she stood in her pastel robe and matching slippers
evoked her own tears. So it was easier to sneak out.

Then it became a game. She'd pack everything
in the car the night before, except for a toothbrush
and a change of clothes, but no matter how quiet
she was, her mother would still beat her to the
kitchen door with a cup of coffee and a kiss. And
that same sad face.

It was more of a challenge sneaking out of the
hotel room without waking up her sister, but she'd
done it. She loved traveling in the dark. It was

always a goal to reach the state line before the sun came up. It gave her something to shoot for instead of feeling sorry for herself. Yes, she was going home to an empty house, but it had always been empty.

Brynn was happy for her sister, she was. Leah now had a reason to get out of that chair. Samuel Fisher was a decent man, who knew what he was getting into and loved her enough to marry her sight-seen. There'd be a learning curve for her sister and perhaps even some rejection from some of the women who considered her an outsider, but there'd be support and fellowship and a man's love.

Then it hit her. They'd not talked about Leah's home in Grand Rapids. It would fall on her shoulders to empty the place. How would she know what to keep and what to donate? Why hadn't this come up in conversation? Because there hadn't been time. According to Ben, all the neighbors on the street shared the shanty phone, so they'd have limited time to talk. And of course, Leah would have to get rid of her phone. Maybe they could talk tonight about what to keep and what to throw. And then there were Leah's bills and her medications. A headache was starting.

It was time to fill up the tank and buy the biggest cup of coffee she could find. As irritation fought to gain supremacy in her mind, her mother's face appeared. *Take care of your sister. Yes, Mom.* She'd keep the promise she'd made to her mother as she held her gnarled hand under the covers as her mom struggled for every breath. Brynn had told her over and over, *Go, Mom. I'll take care of her.*

The sun had been up for hours as she crossed into Ohio. She hadn't realized it was almost three-hundred miles to the state line. Of course, she honked, hoping no one noticed, but the vehicles were far apart. Worrisome thoughts swam through her mind. What if Leah changed her mind and decided she was making a mistake? What if one of her future sisters-in-law shunned her for being English or made fun of the fact that her hands didn't work very well some days, or her feet made her limp? The Amish were hardy people, used to working hard. How could Leah possibly keep up?

All those thoughts took her to Cleveland, and as she sat in traffic, she purposely changed stations in her mind. Enough thoughts of what she couldn't change. Onto Ben. A sense of peace overtook her, and she rested her head back on the headrest. She was probably the only one smiling on I-480W, which had narrowed from four lanes to three due to construction.

She grabbed her phone and tapped on the Bible app called YouVersion and connected it to the pink cable sitting between the seats. With several hours of driving ahead of her, why not start at the beginning and see if Ben was right. She chose Genesis 1 and pressed the oral version. He said that he'd know the answer when he saw it. Would she? Was she astute enough or sensitive enough to hear God's prompt? Busyness had always kept her from listening. Now as she sat amidst a long line of vehicles, she let her mind focus.

The first dozen chapters came and went with no prompt—creation, the fall, the first murder, the flood, tower of Babel, Abraham. All wonderful stories but nothing that told her what to do with her life. She stopped for lunch at a diner near Sandusky at eleven. Maybe listening to the Bible while driving wasn't the best way to discern God's will about selling her motel or marrying Ben. Maybe she should just rely on him to discern God's will.

After a bowl of minestrone and a BLT, she pulled away from the diner for the second half of the trip. Her eyes were tired, but the end was in sight. She'd be home by late afternoon. Her phone rang. Ben. She pressed the button.

"Hi there. How's the trip?" His voice sounded like warm butter.

"Fine. I'm halfway there, and I'll be home around five if all goes well. How's your father?"

"He's doing well. Ornery. They wouldn't let me in to see him at the hospital, but Sam said he has a compound fracture on his right leg, so they have to wait for the swelling to go down, then they'll operate. Then he'll be on a walking cast for the next few weeks. He also has a concussion so they're watching him, but he'll be fine."

"That's good news. So you'll be helping at the farm?"

His sigh bespoke his frustration. "Well, no. All the neighborhood men are gathering to bring in the harvest. So Sam has plenty of help. Neighbors are bringing all kinds of food over so Mamm can be with Daed and not have to cook. It's the way of the Amish."

So wasn't that a good thing? "What's wrong?"

"I was looking forward to spending time with

Daed. There was this tiny opening where he told me to go up to get the cat, and he didn't disagree when I said I'd be there to help Sam."

"Oh, I understand. So if everybody comes together to help him, he won't need you? Is that what you're saying/"

"Yeah. The good thing is for a moment, I saw Daed's heart. *He's* not shunning me." She could hear the catch in his voice. Then silence.

Time to change the subject. "So I've been listening to the Bible on this trip. I'm up to Genesis 14. But I haven't received an answer yet."

"Keep listening. You'll know when you hear it. I'm on chapter 29 today, but I'll read it later after I catch up on my work. By the way, I picked up Leah and took her over to the house. My mother wasn't there, but Sam met me at the car and said Mamm had a guest room ready for her. I guess the wedding's still on."

"Okay…good, I think. Would you ask Leah to call me before she gives up her phone? I don't know what to do with all her things. And I'm sure she has to transfer her bank account and her prescriptions."

"Right. I'll make sure to have her call you. I love you, Brynn. It was great having you here to see my world—as crazy as it is. Let me know." He clicked off.

Let me know. If only God spoke to her the way He did Ben. Maybe she didn't have enough faith. She clicked on the Bible app and turned up the volume. Maybe louder would make her hear it.

The rest of Ohio was filled with the life of Abraham. How could he be willing to sacrifice his son? That was college-level faith, not preschool faith like her own. But God's promise that Abraham's descendants would be as numerous as the stars in the sky could only occur if Isaac lived. But there still was no discernible promise for her.

Brynn honked as she crossed over the Michigan state line. This time cars zoomed all around her. Only three hours to go, and she'd be home. Once she'd unpacked, she'd invite Milli and Brett over for pizza, and she'd give them a generous check to pay for their care of the place.

She was driving past the capital, Lansing, when Abraham's story was almost at an end. He was telling his servant to go to some far place to get a wife for his son Isaac. This sounded like her and Ben's story—two people who lived in different places. The unnamed servant asked, "'What if she refuses to come with me? Shall I bring Isaac to her land?' Abraham said, 'No, if she refuses to come with you, you are released from your oath.'" Was this the message she'd been waiting for? The woman was to move, not the man. She listened on. This had to be it.

Now the servant had traveled to the place, and when he had reached a well, he asked God for a sign. He said, "Let the woman of your choice say to me, 'Drink, and I'll water your camels too.'" Then before he was even finished praying, a young woman said those very words.

Just then, the lane she was in veered off into an exit that she wasn't supposed to take. Cars sped by as she looked for a gap in the traffic. As she moved into the right lane, the narrator's voice grabbed her attention.

"Will you go with this man?" A chill shot down her spine. This was it! "Yes," she said out loud. "I will go with this man." Tears filled her eyes and streamed down her cheeks. Like the servant, she hadn't even reached her house before God gave her an answer. And Brynn knew that she knew this was it.

She turned off the Bible app. Now she needed quiet while she asked God for some kind of confirmation, but she already knew that if Ben would have her, she'd put the motel on the market, climb on her camel, and head to Pennsylvania. Should she call Ben? No, not while she was driving. Give God time to tell her she'd misinterpreted the signs.

Later that night, after she'd finished the laundry, she took a pie she'd picked up at the diner down the street and the check over to Milli's and spent an hour getting an update on the motel.

Then Milli leaned back against her kitchen counter and crossed her arms. "Okay, your turn to spill. I can tell by the sparkle in your eye, something big has happened."

"Leah's getting married. I'll need to go to her wedding in two weeks. How about we close down the place and you come with me? It would be nice to have someone beside me on Leah's side. Two against two hundred Amish."

Her eyes gleamed. "You bet. It will be fun. But you have more to tell, don't you?"

She pursed her lips, not sure if she should say anything. What if she was wrong? "Yeah, I do, but give me some time just to be sure. You'll be the second to know."

Her head tilted. "Second, hmm. What does that mean?"

Brynn stood and pulled her into a hug. "You will know the minute I know. But this is all about God."

Later that night, she took a bubble bath and washed her hair. Funny, normally her television was always on—not to watch but to provide noise for her quiet apartment. But it hadn't even occurred to her to turn it on. She wrapped a towel around her hair and donned her robe. Luckily no one was staying at the motel, so she could go to bed early and sleep late, since no one was there to eat breakfast.

Tomorrow she would do the bills and check on the rooms that were being remodeled, but now cold sheets and a fluffy pillow were all she wanted to think about.

Then a knock on her door made her heart hammer. Who would climb the stairs to her apartment at this hour—nine-thirty? Still, if it were Brett or Milli, they'd call, and she'd already talked to them. Nobody ever came to her place.

It was times like this that she wished she had a peephole. She put her ear against the wood of the door. Another knock made her leap back three feet. "Who is it?"

A male voice. What if it was Jess Cooper with a gun? Maybe she should go to her room and lock the door and call the police. She ran to the window that overlooked the motel road. No truck, just an

SUV—

She ran over and flung the door open. Her mouth hung ajar at the sight. "Ben? What are you doing here?" Grabbing his hands, she pulled him in. "We just talked a few hours ago. How did you get here so fast?" He looked road weary, his hair disheveled. Then her hand went to the towel on her head. What she must look like!

"After I hung up, I started reading. When the door closed for me to help my family, I felt that there was something else God had for me, so I picked up where I'd left off. And there it was. My answer in Genesis 29. 'Then Jacob kissed Rachel and wept aloud.' The minute I read that, I wept aloud. You're my Rachel."

"But I'm Brynn."

"True, but you're Leah's sister, as was Rachel in the story." He took her in his arms, his hands framing her face. "I love you." Then he lowered onto one knee. "Will you marry me? We'll stay here if you wish. Samuel's taken care of now. He and Leah will be baptized. The community will be there for my parents and for my brother."

"Are you sure you want to marry this?" She couldn't have looked worse.

He stood. "You're as beautiful as I've ever seen you. But I'm kind of crazy that way. Marry me, Lady with the towel wrapped around her head."

"Yes, I will. On the way here, I also received my prompt. It was, 'Will you go with this man?' When I heard it, I knew…I just knew. But I didn't call you right away because I wanted to make sure." She summoned a breath, then said, "After I take care of Leah's home, I'll put the motel on the market, and then I will go…with…you."

He rolled his eyes. "You are such a dramatic one. But you don't need to do all that. I kind of like it here—it's a bit more exciting than I'm used to. Seems like a shrink would have his hands full here." With his hand raised, he gazed above her head. "I can see it all now—*Starlite Psychological Services and Motel*.

When she protested that he got the order wrong, he pulled her close, their lips met, and remained. She couldn't tell how long their lips were locked together because she dozed off, or maybe they both did.

The End.

Readers, thank you for reading this story based on my sister's life. If you enjoyed it, please leave an honest review on Amazon or Goodreads. And check out my other books. Sign up for my newsletter, and get in touch if you want to chat.

Sherri Stewart is woman of faith who loves all things foreign and different—whether it's food, culture, or language. A former French teacher, principal, attorney, and flight attendant, her passion is traveling to the settings of her books, sampling the food, and visiting the sites. She savored boterkoeken in Amsterdam for *A Song for Her Enemies*, crème brûlée in Paris for its sequel, *What Hides beyond the Walls*, and shoofly pie in Lancaster for *Tricks and Treachery*. A widow, Sherri lives in the Orlando area with her dog, Lily, and her son, Joshua, who always has to fix her computer. As an author, editor, blogger, speaker, and Bible teacher, she hopes her books will entertain and challenge readers to live large and connect with their Savior. Join, chat, and share with her on social media. Newsletter Facebook Twitter Instagram Website